Miami Noire

A novel

By
W.S. Burkett

RJ Publications, LLC

Newark, New Jersey

The characters and events in this book are fictitious. Any resemblance to actual persons, living or dead, is purely coincidental.

RJ Publications
wsburkett@yahoo.com
www.rjpublications.com
Copyright © 2009 by W.S. Burkett
All Rights Reserved
ISBN **0981777317**

Printed in Canada

June 2009

1-2-3-4-5-6-7-8-9-10-11

MIAMI NOIRE

"The City of Heat "

By

W.S Burkett ©

CHAPTER ONE

Julian

I held her close to me as the smell of blood permeated the room, the same blood that soaked my shirt and covered me in its warmth. Like a rag doll, she lay limp in my grasp. And as I cradled her and mouthed comforting words that surely she couldn't hear, tears streamed down my face.

"Baby, you're gonna be fine," I said, reciting this mantra over and over again; though I had lost all faith in its power the moment I stared into her dead eyes. Selfishly, I couldn't help but wonder what her final thoughts were and if I was one of them.

I saw my father cowering in the corner of my bedroom. He stood with the back of his head pressed against the drywall and a look of fear etched in his wrinkled weather beaten face, the likes of which I'd never seen. It was the look of a man who had just killed the woman he loved. That thought alone caused me more pain. I buried my head into Miko's cold flesh and cried.

From the tears that blurred my vision, I barely saw him jump from my bedroom window. I only heard the shatter of glass and a loud thump. I felt the sting of losing another loved one.

This couldn't be happening. Surely God wouldn't let her life end, not when she was so happy, not when she had a child still inside of her, and not when we realized how much we loved each other. God doesn't like ugly and we did some ugly deeds to get where we were.
You reap what you sow.

Three Years Later...

I hear footsteps. With each step I take, they quicken in pace. I turn around, but no one is there, nor do I know where I'm located. Looking up and down the streets of this unknown town, I'm not able to locate a soul. The streets are dark. The streetlights are losing a battle as they try to flicker, but only leaving an orange glow down their middles.

Once again the footsteps quicken in pace, this time sounding more like a soft jog. Fearing for my life, I take off, my knees buckling beneath me each time my full weight crashed against the concrete. I turn around once more, but still there is no one in sight. I'm running from an invisible predator. The scenery doesn't change. As a matter of fact, each street looks the same, the same houses and the same house numbers. The footsteps go silent, dead silent.

Just as the eerie silence overtakes me, I can no longer breathe. My legs are also rendered helpless. Then a thick gloomy fog befell the area, leaving me blind within inches of my face. The footsteps begin again, this time faster and more deliberate. Feeling paralyzed, I fell to the ground in a heap, for the first time noticing that I was naked.

The hair on my naked body stood on end, as the footsteps got louder. Then the footsteps stopped. Protruding from the fog was a face I'd seen before. Though there were no eyes in his eye sockets, only darkness. There was no denying who it was. There was a gun in his hand. Just as he leaned over with his weapon pointed at my head, a loud vibration swept through the town and he was gone. That was when I woke up. Dripping in sweat, I was happy I made it through another night.

Riches seem so pointless when you have no one to share it with. I owned half of Noire Inc and yet hadn't experienced any heartfelt happiness in sometime. Though there was much to be ecstatic about, part of me refused to feel complete exhilaration. And the other part of my psyche replayed all of Miko's transgressions over and over again. Sometimes I felt as if I was slowly going into a psychotic state.

I lay in a strange bed, the hint of perfume lingering on my flesh, next to a woman I had only met the night before. I barely remembered her name, wouldn't expect to since I only talked to her a total of two minutes before she decided to go to bed with me. This part of my life was swiftly becoming the norm, only a different bed and different face.

That's why I felt so empty inside, sharing myself physically with someone without the prospect of marriage or love was becoming meaningless. Most of the time I didn't sleep with women for need, but instead to cover that gnawing feeling of insecurity that crawled inside of me like microscopic bacteria.

The sound of my phone vibrating on the tiled floor moved me to exit my dazed state. It was my alarm indicating that it was time for me to get to the office. Looking over to my right, I could see that the nameless woman next to me was fast a sleep, so I used that opportunity to disappear into the wind.

I didn't leave a note, no kiss goodbye to end this fairytale. It was what it was and couldn't be packaged any other way no matter how beautiful the gift-wrap.

CHAPTER TWO

Widow

There comes a time in every strong woman's life when you can fall prey to the chauvinistic stereotypes of simple minded men and fall in line with the views of what a woman ought to be. Or you can choose to become like men, unfeeling, unremorseful and unrepentant, answering to no one, but yourself.

Growing up in a very underprivileged household on the outskirts of a small Mississippi town, I learned that I had two strikes as soon as my third generation Haitian-American mother birthed me into this male dominated society. I was black and a female. The black part greeted me every time I walked into a first class establishment I was deemed too second-class to enter into. Short of bleaching my skin, that affliction would always haunt me.

And being a woman, well let's just say I've learned to turn that into a positive. Because of my naturally long legs, flawless, caramel complexion, and the long dark locks that flow down to the middle of my toned back, I've used that to my advantage. Most people mistake me for Angel Lola Luv, but I look better. It's a known fact that a man is powerless in the grasp of a beautiful woman. Even the most astute, disciplined, and educated of the opposite sex possess one fatal flaw, their insatiable appetite of pleasure.

That's why when I walk into a room filled with powerful men dressed in nothing but a simple black dress that accentuates all my curves, giving them a view of my assets, they tend to let their guards down and I introduce them to my insatiable appetite…for pain.

It sounds cruel to say, but I get off on seeing other people hurt, especially those that have hurt my clients. I have never been one to forgive. I can be quite calculating when I want to. In a seconds notice, I'm able to replace the heat of anger that warms my soul into a genuine heartfelt smile in the faces of those that I plan to maim.

For someone so cynical, I'm quite well off and happy with my possessions; though they could never fill the hole in my soul that pushes me to do many of the unfathomable cruelties that I practice. From time to time, they cause me to smile and for those rare occasions, I'm grateful.

Previously, I ran with a crew of narcotics distributors called N.B.D. or *Nothing but Dough*. I was affectionately known as the *Murder Mami* of the clan. Using my sex appeal, I laid waste to their competition. I enjoyed being part of a crew. It was the first time I had any real family in years.

But I made a mistake and fell in lust with the crew's leader and realized I wasn't in a family at all. After he put a price on my head after a botched murder, I decided to take control of my own life. I worked alone and my reputation preceded me. Every crew, making any real money, wanted me on their side. In turn, my wealth grew. As a hired assassin, I lived and killed well.

Pleasure is an all-encompassing word. What provided my pleasure was the fear written on the faces of my victims when they realized they were going to die. The tool of my trade was a knife, a hunting knife with a three-inch blade and gut hook. And as my blade sliced across skin and bone, eventually severing the carotid artery, there was no chance of survival. Though messy, it made each of my murders up close and personal. No one had ever escaped.

In my off shore accounts, I had in excess of twenty million dollars. I also owned a home in Southern California, a small villa in Jamaica, and lofts in New York and Miami. With all that wealth, I had one problem...I wanted more.

I lay in bed with my latest assignment, Joull Guney, a Syrian millionaire, heir to a fabric empire and ecstasy dealer. At sixty years of age and very married, he composed the two qualities that made him utterly attractive. As a mistress, I was kept secret and away from the scrutiny of even his closet confidants. Being the leading ecstasy distributor on the east coast made him powerful, but it also made him vulnerable to competitors. This was business. A very harsh business and he had a price on his head. A price I was going to collect. Joull was a former business partner of my client and I was hired to find his secret stash before gutting him. But after two months of fantastic sex on my part, he hadn't divulged any of his secrets. Yet, I was patient; once he confided in me, he would be a memory.

My real name was Garcelle Jean Louis, but that person died a long time ago in Mississippi, where she was laid to rest. They call me Widow, my calling card being the color I wear, the color of death. Most men never expect me. Too bad they can't peer beyond my eyes. If they could, they'd see nothing but ruin. And my age, well a lady never reveals her age.

The sun just broke from the clouds while I roused myself out of bed. After a couple of stretches and a trip to the powder room I found myself standing at the foot of his bed staring down at him in disgust. For a man that had never done a thing to hurt me personally, I bore such hatred.

Everything about him disgusted me, from his hairy back to his flabby physique. There was nothing physically attractive about him, but it didn't matter. He would meet the same consequences as the others. An Adonis couldn't escape the fate that was destined when I decided that their life was to be taken.

I lay back down in bed, searched for the remote, turned on the television to my favorite show "In the Money" on CNN and was greeted by the face of Miami's hottest developer as he sat on the panel. Among the panelist of disgustingly older men, he shined like a diamond. I sat up in bed and let a smile grow across my lips. Julian Stevens was a sight for sore eyes for he provided me with something I savored, a challenge. Hopefully a beautiful woman dressed in black would be his weakness. Someone with serious bank wanted him dead and after Joull he too would also meet the sharp blade of my knife

CHAPTER THREE

Julian

Sitting nearly thirty stories above I-95 in the lap of luxury of the Wachovia Financial Center in the Miami offices of Noire, Inc., I felt as though I had finally arrived. My office was a reflection of my current state of wealth; I attained the American dream and more with no end in view. Despite the terrible economic climate, we were making profits each quarter. But as the banks held on to their money, I hoped my present situation would stay good and only get better.

A painting from Pat Steir's waterfall series hung prominently next to the doorway. My desk was made from cherry wood and African artifacts were placed meticulously in each corner of my office. This was my haven and had become my oasis; though I owned a twenty thousand square foot mansion, this was my home.

For the opening of my new hybrid hotel, condominium complex, *Miami Noire, was* hosting an event called the "Ultimate Escape" sponsored by Mahogany magazine during Valentine's Day weekend. It was a getaway for the young and sexy crowd, complete with many of the amenities associated with my new venture. One could play on a championship eighteen hole golf course, get pampered in one of our spas, lay out by the infinity edge pool, or eat at the five star sushi bar named after my late wife.

The press we were going to get was vitally important to the success of my business. The event had my undivided attention. There could be no distractions.

"Mr. Stevens, you have a call. It's Mrs. Cumberpatch." My assistant relayed the phone call over my personal intercom as I sat with my legs crossed and my left hand stroking the hairs of my newly grown goatee.

It was a call I actually dreaded, one I promised myself that would never happen again. Mrs. Cumberpatch was my daughter's seventy year old nanny. Once again, I'd left Aasia in her care without so much as a call to inform her that I wouldn't make it home. This was becoming a routine and no matter how much I paid her, I knew in my heart it was only a matter of time before she'd walk out, never to return like the others.

I contemplated my next move, took a sip from my coffee mug emblazoned with the inscription "# 1 dad" in gold and answered the phone.

"Julian speaking," I said quietly, praying that she wouldn't proceed to give me the same tongue-lashing she'd given me just last week for the same transgression.

"Child, I sincerely hope there is a good reason why you didn't let your daughter at least hear your voice before she went to bed. I could barely get her to sleep; she waited by that phone like a lovesick woman. She's too young to be experiencing those kinds of disappointments."

"I'm so sorry; tell her I'll bring her something home tonight. Something special, ask her what she wants."

"The child wants you. She doesn't need material things. That's where you're going wrong. Unless you want a teenager running around showing off her crotch, you'd better start building a better foundation for her." She hissed in her motherly vernacular. Older black women had a way of chastising you without uttering a single vulgarity that pained the heart.

Being selfish wasn't that unusual for me, especially when it came to my daughter. In the tone of Mrs. Cumberpatch's voice, I could sense that it was wearing thin with her, as well. For this reason, there were no excuses. All I could do was bow my head in shame and let my conscience beat me like a runaway slave.

Being a single dad was very difficult, actually more difficult than I anticipated. The good book says that a man that doesn't take care of his family is worse than any sort of man. I always translated that scripture as in providing materially, but I was beginning to realize that it meant more.

"I'll be home early." I took a deep breath knowing that my plate was full at work. "And you can have tomorrow off with pay," I said sincerely as I could, envisioning the smile on Mrs. Cumberpatch's face.

"But before you go, someone wants to say something to you," Mrs. Cumberpatch relayed. I could hear the phone being passed in the background, before the voice of an angel sailed across the receiver.

"I love you, Daddy," my princess said in a heartfelt tone, melting any reservations I had about leaving the office early. "I made a picture for you. It's me, you, and mommy."

Then I realized why it was so hard for me to face my daughter. Lately, she had begun asking questions about her mother. I didn't know why. I figured she couldn't miss or want what she never had, but I was wrong.

"That's nice. I love you too, Beautiful. Tell Mrs. Cumberpatch that I'll call her later."

"Are you coming to see me later, Daddy?" my princess asked. I couldn't give an honest answer, so I hung up without uttering a word.

There was something almost erotic about *The Sports Club/ LA*. On the site of the beautiful Four Seasons Hotel – Miami, it was where the beautiful people roamed. If you wanted to keep in the best shape and be seen at the same time, it had become the spot to be. The setting was the summit of gluttony, with flat screen televisions on each machine and a health food spot not too far away. It provided what only a small few were privy to.

The sounds escaping from the mouths of those working out were orgasmic in nature. The workout machines had become their sexual partners. Sweat dripped down hard bodies while scents of sex lingered in the air. Women dressed in nothing else, but sports bras and tight fitting spandex shorts. It made me feel like I was in the middle east, for there were camels as far as the eyes could see.

Sweat filtered into my eyes, blurring my vision as I grunted in pain, hoping I could finish the last rep of my workout. Soaked in a cesspool of my own bodily fluid as a lay across the weight bench, I struggled to get the barbell from off my chest. My muscles ached, my grip slipped, and at the same time, my resolve dissipated into the funkdafied humid air that surrounded me. Imprisoned underneath three hundred pounds of cold steel, I could only breathe enough to survive.

"You can do it. One more time and you're done. Show me that swag," Frederick yelled into my face while standing over me with his hands tucked over the barbells.

"Take it off. I can't," I grunted, swallowing a mouth full of my own sweat.

"Focus Julian, aren't you a man? This is nothing but steel. You mean to tell me that you can't even conquer this?"

"Forget conquering it. Get this off me," I simmered, feeling the veins popping out of the sides of my neck.

"Act like this is the only thing standing between you and the man that sexed your wife. He's right on the other side of these barbells and he's taunting you." He yelled with more intensity.

I closed my eyes and let my thoughts travel back. Miko overtook my mind. I could nearly smell her and feel her presence. She was in bed with my father, taking in each inch of his love. The whites of her eyes were evident as she stuck her nails into his back with such ferocity that his flesh began to bleed. With that picture in my mind, I opened my eyes and imagined that it was my father on the other side of the barbells.

Like a man possessed, with anger brimming from each pore of my body I slowly pushed the barbells over my head. As I placed it back into its home, I let out a scream and beat my sweaty chest with clenched fists.

"What now? What now?" I declared hysterically, receiving disapproving glares of some in the midst of their own workouts.

"Forget them." Frederick dismissively waved at the onlookers and tossed me a towel. "You did your thing. You are getting cock diesel, boy," he complimented.

"I gotta keep myself in tip top shape. You never know who's gonna run up on you." I wiped the sweat from my face, walked over to my cooler, took out two ice cold bottles of water, threw one in Fredericks direction, and quickly popped the cap on mine.

"Don't tell me you are still worried about Carl," he said while I gulped the refreshing drink down.

"I had a nightmare about that cat last night. I thought I was about to die," I said, wiping my lips with the back of my hand. I trekked back over, sat on the edge of the weight bench, and draped the towel around my neck. "Right after I got my freak on, I see that nutta butta in my sleep."

"Carl did have a tight body. Hell, I had a few dreams about him myself," he joked, staring off into space. I gave him an annoyed look and threw my empty water bottle in his direction.

A few months earlier, I had to fire my company accountant, Carl Samad. I confronted him with a few discrepancies. Later, my out of house auditor found, in our books, that he threatened my life. He returned to work days later with a loaded pistol. If not for the quick thinking of security, I doubt I would even be alive to have nightmares about him.

He was out on bail and I was due in court to testify on March 23rd. I had already received a few threatening phones calls that put me on edge.

"You always have sex on your mind," I stated.

"No, only when I'm awake," he said with his hand on his chin in mock deep thought. "But then again, I dream about sex. So I guess you're right." He laughed tossing his sweat-drenched towel into my midsection.

"Be serious for a minute," I said in a reflective mood.

"I got no time for sentimental stuff. You'll be okay," he said, eyeing the behind of a shapely sista walking by.

"How do you know I'll be okay?" I responded, upset that he would dismiss the seriousness of my situation.

"You are talking to the wrong dude if you want sympathy. You know better than anyone that I can't commit to a relationship, much less conversation. I don't know; maybe I have become desensitized to feelings." He smiled nonchalantly.

Frederick was his father's replica. He could be cold-hearted and charming at the same time. Wealth and good looks allowed him all the excess of life. His partners, whether male of female, were captivated by his brilliant smile, green eyes, and tanned skin. Like a slightly younger version of his father, he gave off an aura of confidence that wrapped a person's mind in it's allure, leaving them defenseless.

"And maybe, that's the reason your relationships don't work."

"Bingo, life is too short to be stressing the little stuff." He patted me on my shoulder. " I gotta go. I gotta lay some pipe before I get back to the office and you know I'm the best plumber in Miami," he said before leaving me with my head down and deep in thought.

Sometimes, I felt I hadn't a friend in the world, but I reasoned that was Frederick's style. He could only be a friend in his own way. No matter how dysfunctional, he was still a dear friend, I hoped.

The atmosphere was engaging; Clarke's was one of my favorite watering holes and I enjoyed its cozy ambiance. Though I looked out of place in an Irish pub it was one of the hottest tickets on South Beach, a place I loved to bring clients and potential clients alike.

But I found myself nursing a whiskey sour in the darkest corner of the bar, wrestling with the idea of going home. For each thought of my daughter, I proceeded to have another drink. Now I was five drinks deep in misery. I ignored each call that Mrs. Cumberpatch placed to my phone. I got a whiff of the most intoxicating scent that I'd ever smelled. A beautiful woman was sitting to my right dressed in a black business suit with a short skirt that rode up her thighs, revealing the most perfect set of legs I had ever seen. Tapping her manicured fingers against the antique wood bar, she stared at me. I could sense that she wasn't used to a man ignoring her. I glanced her way, smiled her way to at least humor her, and then stared back into the glass I held.

"Can't find love in there," she teased in a seductive tone.

"Maybe, but you know what to expect." I sipped from my glass. "And once it's done, it can't come back to haunt you."

"You seem more optimistic in the profile that was written about you in Mahogany magazine. I wouldn't have expected a man of your stature and wealth to drink in order to escape."

"So, you know who I am?" I smiled, thinking that maybe a night of unrequited passion was a done deal.

"I wouldn't go that far. But I can say that I know who you presented yourself to be." She waved the bartender over and ordered a glass of Pinot Grigio, before continuing her piece. "In the article, you said that you had no reason not to be thankful and that your success had given you every reason to want to live a full productive life. I want to know what has changed your mind."

It was humorous how many people felt like they knew you by reading a few well-placed words from a magazine. For some, it gave them the right to judge. And for others, it gave the right to worship. Truthfully though, those types of interviews were just as real as the type of trash you'd pick up at the local supermarket. Who doesn't put on their best face for the world? It was the face behind closed doors that one could never lay bare.

I loosened my tie. I could feel the temperature rising in the room. I let out a soft chuckle and then I put on a serious frown as I turned and faced her. "Funny, you think you know so much about me, but as I recall, you haven't even introduced yourself."

"I'm Andrea Youngblood. I'm a forty year old attorney at Englestein and Associates, single, very understanding and I have a soft spot for sensitive men." She flashed a brilliant smile that would put the radiance of the sun to shame. The bartender returned with her drink. She took a gulp and after barely swallowing, she said, "And I don't want to sleep with you. I only want to be your friend."

This was hardly the type of introduction that I was used to, but she had me wanting more. It was almost like her attempt at putting a halt to any unwanted advances caused me to want her that much more. After more conversation, I learned that she just moved from Atlanta and that she, too, was a widow.

It was that side of her that made me feel more at ease. She really understood what the death of a spouse could do to one's emotions. Not to mention, she was able to put a genuine smile on my face. After talking till closing, I extended my hand. She took it in hers and we shook. "I think I'm going to take you up on that offer," I said. "I'll love to be your friend."

CHAPTER FOUR

Widow

There lies deep dark secrets in my closet. My first murder was committed in self-defense. Yet, the justice system in the great state of Mississippi thought otherwise. I served three years of my life in the Central Mississippi Residential Center for the mentally ill, struggling to understand why I ended up there in the first place. I can still remember the day that I took a man's life like it was branded on my brain and I use that day and those memories to kill…still.

"Momma, you got to take your medication," I said to my mother while she coughed in the kitchen. Sometimes, I wondered if she was being stubborn or plain suicidal.

"I'm alright, Garcelle." She waved me off as I stood in front of her with a syringe full of insulin. "No, you are not." Here, I'll give it to you."

My mother didn't understand all that I had to do in order to afford her medication, without the benefit of medical insurance. We barely had running water in our 12 x 12 trailer, much less money to spend leisurely. Mama hadn't worked since her first stroke. I had to quit school in the ninth grade to work at the local super market and now I made money by dancing at the local bar.

Sullivan's was where I entertained a large group of tattooed red necks dressed in sleeveless t-shirts, trucking caps, and confederate flag bandanas. They called me chocolate bunny and every once in a while slipped in the word nigger as I grinded my behind in their laps. Racial slurs aside, I did it for the money and planned to use that money to get a better life. I kept that part of my life secret from Momma. Finding out what I did for a living would kill my mother quicker than diabetes could ever do.

I didn't care for men touching my body or the alcoholic stench reeking from their skin, but my body was paying the bills. From time to time, I even gave a little more to receive a little more, but never sex, like most of the other girls. Call me old fashioned, but I had dreams that one day my night in shining armor would come and lift me and my mother out of that god forsaken town.

"I'm going to die anyway. So don't worry about me," she said wrapping herself tighter in her favorite plaid robe. She avoided my eyes and stared out the window.

Sometimes, I hoped she wouldn't talk like that. Since my father left, she had given up hope on life. It was as if after fourteen years, she expected him to walk back down that dirt road in search of the hell we lived in. One thing I learned was that men could be so cruel. I also knew there were good men out there that would never leave their wives or children.

"Momma, you'll be fine. Stop talking like that."
Behind blood shot red eyes, she stared at me as if I had offended her. With her index finger up as if she was about to chastise me, I jumped back. But she wasn't going to beat me like I was a child; she imparted words that I live by to this day. "Garcelle, do I look fine?   You got some god damn nerve. Live long enough and you'll learn men ain't worth a god damn."

I didn't truly understand her pain at the time. Sometimes, I wish I did. Most of the time, I wished I could fight her demons for her and carry her pain within my bosom. Maybe that would have preserved her a little while longer, at least until I could have rescued her from her mental agony.
"I'm sorry, Mom." I apologized. I adored my mother. It pained me to make her upset. She pulled me close to her by my sweatshirt. She took my face between her two fragile hands and looked at me with the sort of compassion in her eyes that I had grown accustomed to seeing and said, "Don't be sorry, be wise. Never let a man steal from you what was stolen from me."

Pointing at my heart, she spoke with vigor. "Never let a man steal your heart. It's the only thing you have." Years later, I still lived by those words.

After feeding Momma and persuading her to take her shot, I tucked her into bed and kissed the top of her forehead as she slept. I also said a silent prayer to God to protect and take care of her. Without her, I didn't know what I would do. My dream was to rescue her from that dilapidated trailer that we called home. I prayed that God would keep her breathing until that day.

I counted my money as I prepared to leave Sullivan's for the night. Saturdays were always the best days of the week and I had made enough to pay two months of our past due electric bill and still have a little extra for a nice dress at the thrift store in town. I couldn't stop smiling as I walked the dark tunnel that took us dancers to the secret parking lot.

As I got to the nearly empty parking lot, I forgot that my ride had gotten sick and left early. I couldn't ask any of the other girls, after all the money I had taken in tonight; they would rather see me dead. I took a Newport from my purse and considered my next move. Being a country girl, the trek of two miles to my home was a cakewalk. Equipped with my favorite cashmere sweater, the only expensive article of clothing I owned, I proceeded on my way.

There was a path behind the parking lot that would take me on the main road leading to my home. On a pitch black southern night it wasn't safe to walk close to the road, I stayed far off to the side and prayed that I wouldn't run into a drunken driver or an over eager opossum such as the one I had run into during my youth which nearly chewed my leg off.

I walked about a quarter of a mile when I could feel the heat of someone's high beams behind me. The sound of tires grinding against the dirt and gravel was unnerving. But that sound also told me that whoever was behind me was also slowing down. I moved further to the side hoping that they would get the hint and keep on moving.

"Pretty lady, need a ride?" A deep southern accent of a man's voice hung in the air.

Deciding not to even look in his direction, I waved him off with my hand. Though I was all of nineteen, I was wise enough to know that nothing good could happen at three in the morning.

"You know pretty lady, it's rude to dismiss a gentleman's friendly gesture," he said sounding a little irritated.

His suped up pickup truck pulled to the side of me sitting on what seemed like forty-inch tires. The inside cabin lights were turned on. At that moment, I cursed the low-rise jeans and halter-top I decided to wear that seasonably warm September day. Like my mother, I was top heavy so it was no hiding what I was working with, so with that thought in mind I crossed my arms tightly across my chest.

I glanced in the *gentleman's* direction. I noticed that he was a regular at the club and initially felt relieved. I also knew that the reddish tone of his skin and the glazed-over look in his eyes wasn't attributed to spring water.

We stayed in silence for a while. I walked in a hastened pace and he drove slowly behind me. It was a game of cat and mouse. Finally, after five minutes had passed, and possibly his patience; he spoke.

"Ms., would you rather walk out in them dark woods than accept a ride from me? I'm only interested in getting you home safely. Besides, raccoons can be quite aggressive under the shadow of night."

His statement had grabbed hold of me. Glancing down at the scar on my left leg, I could vividly remember the last time I stumbled upon of one of God's furry creations. I stopped suddenly and so did he by the sound of the screeching brakes. I took a healthy toke of my remaining cigarette. I discarded it, put out the embers beneath my sneakers, and said the hell with it.

"I need to get home. My mother's sick," I said, trying to appeal to his sensitive side.

He was a muscular white man, with a baldhead, ZZ top beard, and a tattoo on the side of his huge neck. He held a wad of chew in his mouth, spitting the remnants out onto the graveled road below. I whispered a silent prayer as I lifted myself onto the stairs and into the truck, practically sitting on a half empty bottle of vodka. I pushed the bottle to the side and placed my favorite sweater over my best asset, my legs.

"See was it that bad?" he said with a smile revealing missing teeth and one stained brown with snuff juice.

"I live on Fairview Ave, right off of Route 51"

"Ohhhh. That's a long walk on these here back roads. You ought to thank your lucky stars that I happened to pass by."

He put the truck in gear and proceeded to drive off. For a moment, all my fears dissipated.

"So pretty lady, cat's got your tongue? Can't give any conversation?"

"No, just have a lot on my mind."

"They say worrying makes you grow old quicker. I ought to know, because I'm only

Twenty-eight years old. And my friends say that I look about forty. What do you think?"
I quickly glanced at him and said, "You look bout your age." I wasn't about to offend
anyone who was doing me a favor, but at the same time, I ascertained that his friends were merely being nice by shaving ten years off his appearance.
The drive was cordial enough as home came into view.
"I get off right about here," I said coyly, belying my initial nervousness, but when those words left my lips so did his chivalry as he stepped on the gas and hit the power locks trapping me inside for what would become hell for the next two hours.

      With terror in my eyes and a fighting spirit, I hit him across the face with all the strength I could muster. He responded with the back of his hand, introducing me to pain and darkness…

      I awoke to excruciating pain; lying on my stomach, I could feel him literally ripping my rectum with each thrust. The barbaric sounds emanating from him were unlike anything I had ever heard. It frightened me along with the pain. I could feel a warm liquid oozing down my leg.

      The full weight of his body was on top of me. If not for a small pocket of space, I would surely have suffocated. I began to struggle. He grabbed a handful of my hair and used it to steady himself, pivoting my head back and almost snapping my neck in two each time he penetrated me forcefully.

Through one eye, I was able to partially see my surroundings. My clothes were scattered about, ripped apart like I'd been attacked by the American werewolf, but something gleamed in the darkness. Attached to the side of his discarded jeans, I noticed a hunter's knife with a serrated edge, the type of knife used to cut the flesh of deer killed for game. My father was an avid hunter and though I barely remembered him, I remember his fascination with knives, a fascination passed on to me.

His sweat rained down upon me. The sounds of his pleasure drowned out my cries of pain.

"You sure is tight missy...," he said, continuing to grunt. "You're as tight as a virgin." He laughed.

His breathing became more labored and his thrusts were longer apart. I could feel his body convulse and his warm orgasm shoot into my body and ooze out of me. Then suddenly he stopped and what I heard next surprised and angered me at the same time. It was the sound of sobbing coming from the mouth of a man that had beaten me, ruined any hope I had of saving myself for my husband, and treated my body like a piece of meat.

The lights of the cabin came on, suddenly blinding me. He took his hands, slapped himself in the face repeatedly, and smashed his skull against the steering wheel.

I cowered against the passenger side door, as my lips quivered uncontrollably. This fear was real. For a man whose emotions ranged from evil to a state of gloom, he could only be crazy. There was no telling what more he could be capable of doing. Fear for my life took control. And that was the reason I reached for that knife. The moment I felt the cold steel against the tip of my fingers, something else overcame me. Fifty stab wounds later, I stood over the body of someone's husband, son, or father. I didn't feel an ounce of remorse.

The look on my mother's face is all I could remember on the day of my sentencing. The judge, an older white male, gave me the maximum sentence for my crime. What should have been self-defense was misconstrued as something else. I was labeled a whore that had taken the life of an honorable family man. If not for my insanity plea, I would have spent life behind the unforgiving bars of a prison cell.

I was hardened from the pain that I had experienced. I didn't want to believe it, but I knew it would be the last time that I'd see my mother alive. And for the third time in my life, a man had dramatically changed my existence. My heart was as good as stolen, for it no longer existed. I decided then as I was led away in shackles that this would be the last.

CHAPTER FIVE

Julian

My Mediterranean styled palatial dream home came into view as I drove through a private gate and navigated down my circular driveway. Tucked in obscurity behind swaying palm trees, highlighted by accent lighting, and stretched across three acres, there was a home fit for a king. My vision of the six thousand square foot oasis had come to reality only a year prior.

Encompassed in my home, there were the usual extras associated with fine living. A red clay tennis court was off to the side, tucked behind the tropical landscape. This is where I got my "Arthur Ashe on" from time to time. Also, on those rare days of relaxation, I loved to float in the infinity pool, which to the naked eye appeared to be sitting on the edge of a long fall. And when I wanted to have the authentic movie experience, I would watch movies on the ten-foot projection screen in my private home theater.

Living my dream didn't help me escape from my demons. My body reeked the stench of whiskey and cigarette smoke of a thousand men. As the garage door opened, I wondered how I managed to get home in my current inebriated state.

As I walked across the travertine tiled foyer of my home, I heard pleasant giggles coming from the family room. With my briefcase tucked securely underneath my arms, I smiled when I was greeted by the smiling face of my daughter as she hopped on the arm of my newly, imported, European, one of a kind, white, leather sectional. Her hands were covered with pink water paint that matched the purple paint that covered her face.

As I glanced at the hands of my Breguet watch, I knew it was hours past her bedtime and though I expected to come home to the intimidating glare of Mrs. Cumberpatch's weather beaten face, I was relieved by the lightened mood, but I was also concerned, because she was nowhere in sight.

Then like a bat out of hell, Frederick came out of nowhere with a frightened look on his face and a dish rag in his hand, headed in Aasia's direction.

"Your daughter's nuts!," he exclaimed as he revealed the pink handprints on his tailored white dress shirt.

I couldn't help but laugh as Aasia evaded him like a pro, squeezing between his legs and finding refuge underneath an accent table.

"Let me get her," I commanded as he tossed me the dishrag, took a seat on a recliner, and let out an exhausted sigh.

"Where's my babysitter?" I asked as I bent down across the lush, snow, tiger, cowhide area rug and fought with my daughter to wipe the pink from her hands.

"Another one bites the dust."

"You mean, she left?" I asked almost surprised.

"She called the office while I was there to check on a site for our next project. She said either I come get Aasia or she was gonna have child services get her instead." Frederick lamented as he wiped at the stains on his shirt. "She said it in no uncertain terms; she also used a couple of four letter words to describe what she thought of your parenting. Your behind owes me one."

I shook my head and cursed myself as I dropped to the sofa with my head in my hands. There was no way I could get another babysitter before tomorrow morning. This wasn't unusual though; I could barely count the number of babysitters I had run through, each leaving with nothing but pity for my daughter. Maybe Mrs. Cumberpatch and the others before her were right. I began to doubt that I could ever become the parent that my daughter deserved.

"Daddy, I'm sleepy," Aasia said, rubbing her eyes.

"Come here. Lay on my lap."

Aasia got from underneath the accent table and she sat beside me with her thumb in her mouth. She rested her head in my lap and she instantly fell asleep. I looked down at my daughter. I looked into the face of pure innocence. I wondered if she would struggle in this world as I had struggled. My love was unconditional, but I couldn't protect her from the harsh realities of life. That thought, in of it self, troubled me and it was probably what made me so hands off. The thought of seeing innocence vaporize like it had never existed was my worst fear, for I had seen it in her mother.

Hours after carrying my daughter to her Dora the Explorer themed room, Frederick and I found ourselves huddled over by my personal wet bar, doing shots of tequila and talking only as deep as two drunken men could. The room was dim, only the slow burn of candles revealed my presence and the aroma of Miami's finest hash permeated the room.

"You know, I miss my father," Frederick slurred after taking another shot to the head, followed by a toke of a rolled joint. Living a carefree debauched lifestyle was his thing; though it interfered with his work, it was who he was.

I attributed his statement to the buzz he'd acquired. Since he'd taken over his forty five percent share of the company following his father's death, we'd barely even spoken Darren's name. That subject was one topic I didn't want to speak on, so I just nodded my head and hoped this moment would pass.

Over the past three years, Frederick became family. Other than my daughter, he'd become the only other stable person in my life. Dreading that my hand in his father's death would come to light, it kept me from ever reminiscing of the past.

Tears built up in the corner of his eyes. His body trembled with force as he silently wept.

"Do you know that I wasn't even on speaking terms with him before he died?" Frederick cried.

Avoiding his eyes and keeping my glare on the contents of my glass, I patted him on the shoulder and reassured him. "You aren't the only one. I had to watch as my father's body was peeled off the concrete."

I tried to let my own tears fall. I struggled to join my friend in his moment of grief, but my own tears revealed my true feelings. The thought of my own father didn't bring anguish. Instead, it brought anger.

"If only he could have seen the man that I'd become... He would... really be proud of ...Miami Noire." He sobbed.

Once again, silence overtook us. In the midst of silence, truth is told. Silence spoke more than a thousand tongues could ever enunciate.
"You two were close. Did he ever speak of me? Did he even care?"

Not knowing what to say, I went into deep thought like anyone who had to lie. "He always spoke of you. He loved you." I said as eloquently as possible.
"I hated him for years, hated that he left me and my mother. Sometimes, I would wish him dead." I squeezed his shoulder, trying to help him shrug the liquor that was causing him to speak things that he didn't mean. "No Julian, I'm serious. But what I hated most was that he saw you as a son and not me." His statement caused a chill to go up my spine, besides the first time that I had met him, he'd never shown any type of disdain towards me.
"Darren always knew you'd do fine. He said it was in your character." Beneath my hand, I could feel his muscles begin to relax. Like that, the moment had passed.

Looking at Darren's spitting image, I couldn't help but wonder if they shared any other traits - like the thirst of blood or the lack of loyalty, all trademarks of Darren's character. But like a true friend, I wanted to protect him from the truth. Sometimes, there was no place for the truth. At that moment, I knew if I'd told him all that his father was, he'd go off the deep end. I squeezed my arm around him tightly and hoped that he'd never know who Darren Edmonds really was.

CHAPTER SIX

Widow

In the morning when I opened my eyes, Joull placed a tray of food before me, complete with mango slices, whole-wheat waffles and my favorite egg white omelet. It wasn't until he placed the Tiffany's box on my bare stomach that I decided to spend the day with him. After a night out on the town scouting my next assignment, I wanted to sleep all day, especially after my discovery, but my greed got the best of me.

I had to admit to myself that I looked fine. Staring in the passenger side mirror of Joull's banana yellow Aston Martin Vantage, I could barely hold in my admiration. My hair was free, flowing down to my back and blowing in the wind as we rode up Collins Avenue with the top down. My beauty even made Joull a little more bearable for the eyes.

Even on a hot summer day, I enjoyed dressing in black. Like the harlot sister of the Grim Reaper, I took great care in never drifting too far from my look. I wore a black Dolce silk chiffon blouse with cascading front ruffles, a pair of low-rise, black, skinny jeans over my shapely backside, and finished my refined style with a pair of oversized Dior sunglasses, all were gifts from Joull.

When I awoke this morning, I considered finishing what I had come to do, but I hadn't gotten the word. I'd found his stash; it had been right under my nose, hidden in the basement of his home, tucked behind insulation. I was able to put away a hundred thousand for a rainy day, unbeknownst to my client.

"Baby, I'm gonna make you happy today." He smiled as he slid his hairy hands up my thigh. To him, I was nothing more than a replication of "Pretty Woman". He took great gratification in flaunting his extravagant taste.

"It's so beautiful, Joe," I said with a flighty tone in my voice. Playing the role of his virtuous paramour was right up my alley.

Though the scenery before me was exciting, I couldn't help but think about what would be coming shortly. I took a sadistic pleasure in controlling the life span of my victims. Knowing full and well that I could cut it short at any moment; got me off. The surprised look in the eyes of my victims, as they gasped their last breath, was comparable to an orgasm.

After parking the car and surveying the scene for any sign of his wife, Joull grabbed my hand and proceeded to show me around the perfectly kept grounds of Bal Harbour Mall. In his mind, this was a maiden voyage for my Christian Louboutin's, but it was not. I'd come to take in the landscape of Miami's most upscale location many times before. Unbeknownst to him, this was the place that I'd first noticed him. It was my scouting location and he practically lived there. I never left anything to chance, knowing a person's routine served me well.

Bal Harbour Mall was a splendid location exhilarating for the senses. The aroma of the ocean breeze coming in from the beach aroused me. It gave me images of walking nude in the wet sand with a man I actually loved. The sound of water forming in surrounding fountains was a lullaby to my tired soul. And the lush foliage and palm trees compared favorably to what I had imagined the Garden of Eden to be.

I remember the very first time I had distinguished Joull among all of this beauty. He was strolling along the concrete walkway with his wrinkled, orange tinted wife, both advertising looks of despair. My superior ability of perception told me that he toiled in a sorrowful marriage, but by the jewels his wife displayed on her body, I also knew he was well off. It wasn't long before he'd moved me into his second home and he was coming home to me every night.

The only thing that attracted me to Joull was that he exuded power. Powerful men were my weakness, especially powerful bad men. He walked into a room with such confidence that he intimidated anyone in his path. He dressed like a late eighties style mobster and played the part. Today he looked more Tony Soprano than Millionaire. He was dressed in gray slacks and a red silk shirt buttoned down low enough to expose the hairs on his chest. There existed nothing he couldn't get if he wanted and what he wanted was to make me happy.

As we entered Harry Winston, I couldn't help but gaze admirably at the display of diamonds before me.

"It's beautiful in here," I said, looking back at Joull for his approval

"Go, go. Look. I buy," he said in his choppy English, with a broad smile on his face revealing a set of teeth dulled yellow by a habit of cigar smoking.

The moment we walked in, I noticed the twinkle in the eye of one particular sales woman. Though she fit right in with the clientele of the store, her eyes told me two things. She was either greedy or hard on her luck. I leaned more towards thinking she might need the commission. My life had taught me to decipher a person's true intentions. Besides being the only other sista that I had noticed in the entire mall, I figured buying something expensive would help her out.

"That looks nice," I said, pointing down at a pair of beautiful chandelier diamond earrings set in platinum.

"You have great taste," the sista said in her best white girl imitation voice. She walked over and extended her hand towards Joull and I. "I'm Natalie and you are?"

"I'm Brittany and this is my *man*." I made sure to emphasize the fact that he was mine. I didn't need to be pushed aside before my purpose was complete.

I'd be blind or plain lying if I was to say that she wasn't attractive. Hell, she was much more than attractive. Not only did she have the physique of a model, she also had pin straight hair flowing down to her back, ending at her protruding posterior. With plump lips and almond shaped eyes, there was no denying that she was mixed with something else. But with an expensive pair of earrings on her ears, an expensive suit covering her frame and with manicured hands, she appeared too well bred for Joull's taste. Men hated women that didn't need them.

"It looks pretty and much too expensive," I lamented, fully knowing the thought of buying me the earrings would put Joull's ego in overdrive.

"I think I know you Mr. Guney," Natalie said, forging ahead of me.

"I'm sorry, Miss. I'm Joull," Joull responded by taking her slender hands in his as a reddish glow covered his cheeks. "My memory fails me sometimes."

First, I sized her up, and then glanced in Joull's direction. I wondered if I could notice a glint in his eye that would tell me whether or not she was something he would want for himself. But like any lovesick fool, he only had eyes for me. He proved this by releasing her hands and grabbing my hand even tighter.

"Get it out. Let us see," Joull directed as the woman quickly retreated behind the display counter and unlocked its contents.

There was never a more beautiful sight. The diamonds sparkled as she placed them up to my ear. I took one in my hand, twirled it around with my fingertips, and inspected each fleck of its brilliance as it hit the sunlight. I could barely contain the broadening smile on my face from revealing itself.

"Could you please wrap it up? I'll buy," Joull said, grabbing a handful of my behind as I delightfully squealed.

I could feel the judgmental gaze of my sista beaming down on me as Joull walked away to answer an important phone call on his blackberry, leaving behind only his American Express card to keep me company. As she situated herself behind the register, I decided to confront her.

"What's the problem?" I asked, while still surveying the other jewels on display.

"Nothing. I was just wondering how you snagged someone so generous."

"Well, what business is it of yours?" I shot her a deadly look and prayed she wouldn't push for fear that she'd become my next victim, instead of Joull.

"I'm only giving you your props, girl," she joked, losing her white girl vernacular and replacing it with a dialect straight from Little Havana.

Slowly but surely, I was certain that she spotted my game a mile away. I wasn't sure where our conversation was going, but before I snapped on her, an idea crossed my mind that even made me smile.

"I'm sorry, girl. You know how people are. But the truth is, it takes no skill to get a man like that," I said, peering at the five-figure price tag on the earrings as Natalie calculated the total on the register.

"Maybe not for you. But finding a man that wants to do anything for me is hard. I've had my fair share of dogs." She smiled. It was becoming quiet evident that this girl had low self-esteem. She needed a little confidence.

Since she was simply gorgeous, her looks rendered her too intimidating or unapproachable for even the most confident man. But she seemed like the type of woman that didn't know how use her greatest assets. Without knowing her, I could tell that she gave much too much and received little in return. Natalie was possibly a former ugly duckling that grew into a beautiful swan and she didn't even notice the transformation. One single principle eluded her. Men only want what they can't totally conquer.

"I'm not trying to hit on you. But with your looks, if you applied a few well placed principles, you'd get more than you could ever dream of."

"You think."

"I know."

After telling me her history, I learned that she was much more similar to me than I thought. A silver spoon had escaped her at birth, as well; she toiled through poverty while growing up in foster care, going from home to home. Living life without a family put her at a disadvantage. She had no one she could totally trust. Nigerian born, she'd been ridiculed in ways most people could barely fathom. Toiling between dead end retail jobs and worthless men, she had the insatiable urge to get ahead.

She put my gift into a small velvet box, placed the box into a small bag, and handed it to me.

"Can I get your number?" she asked and I handed her my card containing my personal phone number, as Joull sauntered back into the store like a bull. One unnerving though crossed my mind; the possibility that my motives were transparent scared me. What next? Was my past catching up with me?

"Natalie. Have we met before?" I had to ask, trying to remember her face from my mental Rolodex.

"Yes."

"When?" I smiled as nervous energy worked its way up my spine.

"You don't remember me?" She asked, staring intently. I tried to make out her face.

"Sorry, I don't remember."

"I remember you… Garcelle," she replied with an all-knowing smirk. Time began to slow; in my mind I knew it wasn't possible. No one knew who I really was, no one. The possibility caused my stomach to churn. And then I remembered her face, it became clear as day. Instantly my legs gave out and I dropped to the floor. The world became a blur.

CHAPTER SEVEN

Julian

Right before my eyes, there lay a sea of white and red shirts and jerseys. The aroma of freshly baked pretzels, popcorn and mustard drenched hotdogs filled the atmosphere. The roar of anticipation filled the United Airlines arena as a group of scantily clad, subtle breasted Miami Heat dancers shook their thang on the hardwood floor. Their bodies were like instruments, playing in harmony with the thumping beats booming from the speakers.

Always the embodiment of a basketball fan, this afternoon I looked like one of the players dressed in an official Miami Heat jersey, red rip away sweats and a pair of the new Dwayne Wade converse sneakers.

I managed to sneak away for the night knowing that my daughter was in good hands. I left her with my next-door neighbors. This was a no-brainer. They were an interracial couple that wanted children of their own and had volunteered to watch Aasia many times before. After the abrupt departure of Mrs. Cumberpatch, I finally took them up on their offer. They'd grown quiet smitten with my princess. Though the task of procuring her next babysitter wasn't going to be easy, at least my mind would be at ease for the night.

The place was jumping, but my partner in crime looked like someone he loved had left him. With the appearance of a scorned man, Frederick didn't look the least interested in the event. Slumped on a plush leather sectional in a secluded corner of my sky box clutching his third Hennessey and coke, with his tie hanging haphazardly around the side of his neck, he looked dejected and I wondered if he was still thinking about his father.

"Freddie, you look like someone shot, kicked and molested your dog," I said, heading in his direction.

"Nah, I'm cool. I'm just trying my best to chill," he responded in an icy tone that reeked of contempt.

After spending so much time with Frederick, I learned how to decipher his moods and temperaments. There was much more to his ornery demeanor than plain relaxation. With all the long hours that he put in at the office, I wondered if his personal life was suffering. So I decided to press on further, at least to see if I could be of any assistance.

"Having man or woman problems?" I pried, though the cutting action of his eyes as I hovered over him told me to ease up. Frederick was of the liberalist belief that love was love and sex was sex, no matter the sex of his chosen partners.

"Neither one. Can I have some time to myself?" He demanded, his voice trailing off as T.I's newest single played on his phone. He didn't budge; instead he decided to let the phone serenade him until it went silent.

"Well, you look pissed off, so I'm gonna bug you until you let me in," I said taking a seat beside him as I gave him a playful jab to his midsection

Finally figuring there was going to be no other alternative, he decided to speak. He sat up straight and twirled his body in my direction, so that we were face to face. He said, "I want more input on the next project."

I didn't know how to counter. Our business relationship was clear. I designed the bigger projects, dealt with the lawyers, brokers and investors, while he used his real estate expertise to handle the general contractors and zoning agencies. He showed a keen eye for details that proved to be an asset. But the inability to commit to anything was his main adversary. His interests blew like a leaf in a typhoon storm and so did his emotions. Sometimes he came to work like he was on a mission. Other times, I could barely reach him. It depended on the type of hold his new lovers had on him. Once, he ruined a project that I planned to purchase in Los Angeles County by showing up to a meeting with drunk investors. I didn't take him seriously when it came to the future welfare of my company.

"What type of input are we talking about? We've had this conversation before and you remember the outcome of that experiment," I reminisced, while speaking with candor.

"My father founded this company. And I think it's only right as his son that I do something to cement his legacy and the Edmond name."

I could feel the vein in my forehead begin to swell. I felt my heart quicken in pace as I began to sweat. My mouth felt as if a desert lived in it and my stomach did laps that the likes of Michael Phelps couldn't conceive. At the same time, it felt as if my blood was coming to a slow boil.

We were in the beginning stages of development of our next Noire project. With the great press Harlem and Miami Noire had garnered, I wanted our next site to set the Noire brand further apart from all other boutique hotels, but getting the needed backing was becoming nearly impossible. As the country hit a recession, the hotel business suffered and no one wanted to take a chance on Noire, Inc.

"When we find a site then we'll go from there," I stated, hoping that my statement would end the discussion.

"I've already found one. All the property acquisition costs and fees look reasonable. I've also found equity funding from a few investors that would greatly decrease the need for exorbitant out of pocket costs," he stated with such confidence that I couldn't help but be impressed.

That explained his long hours in the office and his insistence. Frederick never struck me as the sort of guy that thrived under pressure. It often seemed that he loved owning a company but not the work that went along with it. At the same time I felt a rush of hypocrisy for even rushing to judgment. Maybe his idea would be worth considering.

The old saying "love at first sight" was so cliché that I didn't know how to explain my feelings as I watched Andrea walk to my car, down the winding driveway of her home. Wearing a tight fitting, black, strapless dress that ended inches above her knee, she provided indication of where her paradise lived. It gave me proverbial butterflies.

The dress, though revealing, displayed the best attributes of her physique. With thick thighs, unyielding breast, and a behind that peeked around the front, she had me in awe. Her hair was set in natural wild curls and all the right parts of her bounced, as she walked towards me with the ease of a pro in five-inch stilettos.

Hopefully, I wouldn't be a gnat cast in her gorgeous shadow. I endeavored to appear relaxed as I sat in the bucket seat of a newly purchased cherry red Maserati. Sporting a powder blue, Prada, v-neck sweater with faded blue seven jeans and sandals, it was a look that down played my anxiety.

For the first time in years, I looked forward to spending an expectation free evening with a woman. Sex wasn't on the menu. This was indicated during my call to her from my skybox earlier that evening. Becoming one with her was the furthest thought from my mind. Our last encounter had left me wanting more, wanting to know more about the mysterious woman in black. If anything, I wanted to know what made her tick.

Blazing a trail from her home to our destination, the drive took me less than half an hour. We made small talk, but I hoped she would open up a little in the coming hours. Though it was nearly ten o'clock when we arrived, I looked forward to our night together and all that it entailed. I had reserved a bed at a Miami club of the same name.

All eyes were directed towards us as we entered B.E.D and I basked in the scrutiny. Not only were we allowed access into one of the hottest destinations in all of Miami Beach, but we were a couple to be reckoned with. Being seen with her boosted my confidence into the stratosphere and I hoped the feelings were mutual. I thought we were made for each other and by the end of the night, I was sure she would feel the same.

The club's intimate vibe had me wrapped in a cocoon of sensuality. White curtains cascaded down from the ceiling. We were surrounded by white walls washed in purple light. Orange scented candles were situated in the middle of all the oversized beds. The D.J. spinned all the most popular hits as the crowd navigated to the open bar. Alcohol and music were a potent mixture.

Andrea held onto my arm as we parted the crowd. The anxiety that lived in her body was evident by the way she tightly clung to me. I could tell that she didn't like being the center of attention, if even for a moment. And there was no denying that she was in the spotlight. As the eyes of every man rested on her voluptuous assets, I reveled in their desire. With a slight touch of her waist, I had claimed victory.

Andrea released my arm as soon as we were seated and nervously inspected the entire scène.

"Looking for someone?" I mentioned nodding my head to the newest T-Pain hit.

"I'm really anal when it comes to knowing my surroundings," she claimed, pulling at her hair. Though, I didn't believe her, I decided not to interrogate her any further. I just hoped there weren't any crazed ex-boyfriends that she conveniently hadn't mentioned.

Minutes later, after our orders were taken, we both got more comfortable by removing our shoes. I thought it would be the ideal time for meaningful talk.

"Can I ask you a question?" I probed. Because of her sitting position, her already short dress had ridden up her thighs, far enough that I could see the black fabric of her panties. I could barely take my eyes off her special place as I wondered what was on the other side of the fabric.

"The answer isn't between my legs," she interjected while crossing her legs and placing a handkerchief on her lap. My face went flush, because of my light skin. My embarrassment undoubtedly had probably turned my face crimson red.

After composing myself, I asked her, "Have you gone on a lot of dates since your husband's passing?"

She looked away into the distance. I could tell she wasn't really looking at anything in particular. She seemingly was in deep thought, most likely looking at something in her mind's eyes. The disco light above us reflected off her eyes, revealing that they were now glazed over. Instantly, I felt ashamed that I'd even ventured off into that territory. Grief, for some, always stayed fresh and for others, was only a thought away.

"I apologize. I didn't mean to bring back any bad memories." It was as if my words allowed her to release the tears that were pent up inside.

"Thank you," she replied while wiping the tears from her eyes with the handkerchief that had graced her lap.

She gave no further explanation. Compassionately, I let it be. I didn't want to probe into uncharted territory for there was no telling what I'd find. Her guard was up; thus my only alternative was to gain her trust.

"What sort of law do you practice at Englestein and Associates?" I was interested in her true passion. I wanted her to know that my interest went further than what was between her spectacular legs.

The waitress arrived with two entrees of Caribbean lobster baked in pineapple, celery, and tomatoes. She placed the plates in front of us. She filled our glasses with Moet Chandon Rosé and left as swiftly as she arrived.

Andrea composed herself. She wiped at the remnant of tears cascading down her sharp cheekbones and smoothed out her dress before crossing her legs once more. As the steam from the lobster filtered up into her nose, she closed her eyes and bowed her head in prayer. I did the same, but I didn't pray for the food; instead, I prayed that our night would only improve.

"I practice entertainment law," she said opening her beautiful hazel eyes. She took a fork full of the succulent lobster tail, opened her mouth, and enjoyed the taste. The allure of her lips overtook me. The way they protruded in fullness at the bottom made me wonder how they would taste.

"You represent anyone I know?"

"Probably, my clients include a few ball players and singers." With a protective wave of her finger, she continued. "But I believe in client confidentiality."

Though, she would have never known, I respected her response. It showed me that she was a woman of integrity. In this day and age, that was hard to find. Most women let their morals go and instead, adopt the attitude of the men that disappointed them. Gone were the days when all women upheld standards that a few men couldn't.

We rained quietly as we indulged our appetites. The food had no comparison and the champagne went down smooth. I could eat nor drink any more and by the content expression on Andrea's face, I could tell she had relished the array of flavors that had exploded into her mouth. "Forty years young and you are already a partner," I said in awe.

She couldn't help but let a smile escape her stoic expression. The thought of what she'd accomplished made her happy and it was a pleasure to see.

"I still have a lot to learn," she humbly admitted.

"Like not being so modest..." I returned the smile. I looked directly into her eyes but she looked away. That worried me, because her avoidance of eye contact told me either she didn't trust me or I couldn't trust her. There was something obviously on her mind. She wasn't that ultra confident woman that I'd met at the bar. She took her last bite of lobster, put her fork down, wiped her mouth, and washed it down with champagne. The waitress returned, removed our plates, and took our orders for the open bar.

"Are you feeling alright tonight?" I asked.

"Just a little burned out at work. I'm struggling with a big case," she admitted.

"You love the law? Only the most focused brought work home with them…"

"It's not like I'm handling life or death cases, but I believe in doing the best that I can for the welfare of my clients. I get what they want."

"I'm sure some of them just want you," I complimented.

Her body language compromised her feelings. She shook her head, rolled her eyes, and balled up her napkin before tossing it to the table.

"I hope my clients take me as seriously as I take my job. Hopefully, my appearance has no bearing on my job performance."

Like a fool, I'd insulted her. My lack of recent dating experience was transparent. I possessed very little skills in the art of seduction. In the last three years since my star had risen, outside of asking a woman if they were on any birth control, there were no other reasons to ask questions about their personal lives. Mostly, because I didn't care and now that I did, I didn't know how to put it into words.

"I'm not misogynistic. It's just that some men can't see anything past a woman's outward appearance," I commented. She didn't say a thing. Instead, she remained silent as she collected her thoughts.

In our world, there's a double standard. And like the average Joe, I'd done nothing to dispute it. Most men see a beautiful woman and feel it's their right to objectify them. For some, all chivalry goes out the window and replaced by a cave man like mentality. But I was different. Still, though I held women in high regard, I'd done nothing to show otherwise. Even when Frederick treated them impersonally, I'd done nothing.

"Julian, I'm not trying to accuse you of anything. But I've dealt with sexist men since the day I began to develop. They are the reason it's harder for me, as a woman, to be taken seriously. I'm beautiful, thus, that's all I'm worth to some. Perception is reality."

The tribulation in her eyes spoke to me. Like a film, it showed years and years of disappointment at the hands of men. That was when I realized that before me was a person that didn't need a knight in shining armor nor did she need a man with riches or one who could satisfy her sexually. She needed someone she could trust. The only way to gain her trust was to put my own insecurities on the line.

I reached across and massaged her fingers. Giving a peace offering, I let her know that I felt for her and for what all women, especially those of color, went through. Next, I told her my fears.

"I feel the same pressure, as well. I'm a man, but I'm a black man. What bothers me is that we have to work so much harder to get ahead. Even in my line of work, no matter the success I have, it's still difficult to convince others to invest in me and my vision. Now that banks are failing and money is tight, it gives people a reason to discriminate. Sometimes, I want to say the hell with living the right way and being an upright citizen," I reasoned as I removed my hand from hers and lay across the mattress.

"Don't let them jade you, brother. We need brothers like you in the board rooms, so other young men get a shot."

"All of our young men look up to sports stars or musicians. I'm a square to them," I reasoned, though feeling guilty about making that sort of wide ranging statement.

This was something unique. The dialogue between the two of us wasn't normal chitchat. But rather, it was the exercising of fears that most black professionals experience. We were either discriminated against in corporate America or ostracized in our own communities for being successful. My father always said that I was trying to be a big shot just for trying to be more than he could be. He never knew how his fears could have limited me.

Andrea loosened up. Her attention was on the dance floor. The music overtook her. Our drinks finally arrived. Good food and great music was the best antidote for grief. I watched as she took a sip of her apple martini and nodded her head to the beat while swaying her glass from side to side.

We gave puzzled looks to one another when we noticed a couple out on the dance floor nearly having sex. And they had to be black. The brotha's face was halfway up the sista's skirt as she did a new take on the tootsie roll. The fingers from both his hands were between her butt cheeks as he savored her scent. They had everyone's attention as the D.J. began to spin reggae hits.

"Some people just don't have any class." Andrea sneered, giving the couple a fatal glare. "You can get your groove on without being tacky."

"How do you think you got here?" I exaggerated. "Let them have their fun."

"Your parents would slap the black off you if they heard you say that." She continued staring at the couple as if she had eaten something sour.

I put my arms up and shrugged my shoulder. "Hey they aren't alive to dispute it. They are both long gone."

"You must be fascinated with death. Every so often, you seem to stick it in our conversation,"

She queried, finally taking her eyes off the dance floor and directing her attention to me.

Admittedly, I'd seen so much death around me that I tended to be preoccupied with it. After the passing of my mother, death seemed to always be in my midst. With the death of Miko, Darren and my father's death hung over my head like a dark cloud. It was something I expected and since the start of my nightmares, it became something I could visualize.

"I wouldn't say that I'm fascinated. But it's a fact of life," I debated.

"Some people die long before they are laid to rest. And some bring death to themselves. Have you learned anything from 2 Pac?" she asked.

"I live. This right here is living," I said, scanning the club for effect.

"No, you're existing." She took a sip from her martini, extracted the olive from the glass with a toothpick, and twirled it in her mouth seductively before swallowing.

"And what about you?"

"What about me?" she said indignantly.

"Mrs. Have No Fun…"

"So, you think you know me?" Her voice rose. I could tell I was one insult away from a tongue-lashing and I wasn't going to go there.

"You don't let your guard down."

"What do you want to know?"

"I want to know about you, about your life. Where are you from?"

"Didn't I tell you everything about me at the bar?" she said, taking another sip from her glass.

"Refresh my memory." I wanted to understand her, wanted to know what made her human, and what made her laugh or cry. "I talked about my family, but tell me about yours."

"My mother's dead and I don't remember my father," she recounted quickly. "There it goes. Now, do you feel like you know me?" She rolled her eyes and threw her hands up in the air.

"What about your husband?"

"What about him?"

The alcohol she'd consumed was bringing out her wild side. The guard she brought into our date had fallen. I thought it was no better time than at that moment than to tell her about my daughter.

I dug into my jeans, took out my wallet, and extracted a picture of Aasia. I wanted her to see the most important person in my life. I wanted to show that death wasn't the only thing on my agenda.

"This is my princess." I handed her the wallet-sized photo of my daughter, as I looked for her reaction. There was no way she'd know I had a daughter. In all my press I made it my duty to keep my daughter a secret.

"Awww. She's so cute," she said, holding the picture delicately between her fingers. "She must get her looks from her mother," she jabbed.

Though her intended purpose was to humor me, I couldn't help but be saddened by that statement; for I couldn't see my likeness in my daughter's face. Often, because of Miko's exploits, I wondered if she was even mine.

"Do you baby-sit? Or represent any nannies? I can't seem to find one," I joked.

"No, kids don't like me, but there's an agency called "Children R Us" that caters to professionals like yourself." She stared into my eyes intensely and with pity. "I'm sorry for joking around. I can see you in your daughter's eyes."

When Andrea put her hands on mine, I felt heat. With her simple touch, I was electrified. She invigorated something inside of me. But all I could do was sheepishly smile and hide the pain within.

"I got an idea." She stood, hiked up her skirt a little and grabbed my hand nearly pulling me from the bed. As I got up, she pulled me close enough that I smelled the apples on her breath.

"What do you have in mind?" I asked nervously, not sure what the sinister smirk that had spread on her face was all about.

"Let's show them how it's done with class." She pointed towards the couple still having intercourse on the dance floor. Andrea took charge grabbing my hand and leading me out onto the dance floor.

Once again, she had me spinning. This wasn't what I would've expected from a prim and proper attorney. That spontaneous facet of her personality continued to have me on edge.

When we got on the dance floor, she led me into a dark corner of the club where we would have privacy. On the smoky dance floor, we danced to rhythms of Maxi Priest's "Close to you". Holding on to her waist, we danced as one. Her hips guided me and the noticeable girth of my manhood seemed to excite her as she gyrated up and down its length.

The sounds of the Caribbean, at that moment, provided a soundtrack to my life. Everyone on the floor danced closely and with a carnal passion. Bodies perspired, as the temperature seemed to rise with each move. Andrea glowed. Her skin glistened with a layer of sweat while I watched her booty wind. She turned around, grabbed my waist, and we locked lust filled expressions as the music hypnotized us. It felt like making love and I hadn't felt that in some time.

There was no better moment to make a move, so I did. I brought her close and placed a tender kiss on her collarbone. Her eyes closed and a moan escaped her lips. I put my hand on her thigh; it had been tempting me all night, so I needed its touch. She continued to wind until we were in a tight embrace, while my hand continued to ascend up her thigh in search of the black fabric. I was well within inches of her opening when she brought her lips to mine and we hungrily kissed. Now we'd become that couple that we judged earlier. Caught up in the throes of passion, I barely felt it when she bit into my lip and broke the skin. She didn't even recoil and as I tasted my blood, she did, too.

"Damn," I said in horror, pulling away with my hands over my lips.

"It's time to go." She wiped her face with the back of her hand and lowered her skirt. Embarrassment had consumed her. Thus, she walked away and back to our bed to gather her things; then she went out of the front door, disappearing into the night.

CHAPTER EIGHT

Widow

After my tumble to the floor at Harry Winston's, Joull treated me to a deep tissue massage at the Agua Spa in the Delano Hotel. I was spending so much time at one of Joull's mansions that I had been neglecting my own place. His wife didn't care that he never seemed to be home with her. That was fine by me, because I received word to take care of him. I needed absolute privacy.

Though his sex game was lousy, his attentive nature was slowly making me soft. I couldn't have that. When a person becomes soft, that's when they make mistakes. I had learned that lesson once before. The truth of the matter was that he was a heartless cheat. His death would be my gift to his wife.

Agua was a beautiful oasis where I came to relax. Situated on top of the Delano, it provided the most beautiful view of the Atlantic and South Beach's splendid landscape. When I needed to relax, it was where I came. It gave me the opportunity to think. And at the moment, I had a lot on my mind, like where I'd met Natalie.

Natalie Robinson was her name and we were roommates at Central Mississippi State

Residential Center. As the only two blacks, we became fast friends. She was overweight in the past. That was the reason that I barely recognized her at Winston's. The meds and fatty foods she was consuming had made her nearly obese. At the time, her appearance didn't matter to me, because she seemed genuinely interested in my welfare. She protected me from the lustful stares of the other women, while helping me endure many tear filled nights, nights when I told her things I had never told anyone.

But Natalie was sick and quickly became obsessed. She had started to write me notes about her undying love for me. Once, she even tried to go down on me while I slept. I was flattered at first. But I didn't want to hurt her then; my sympathy caused me to be blindly loyal, so I played along. She was into women and I respected her sexuality, but it wasn't for me, so I sheepishly fought off her advances. We shared a kiss here and there, but I left never expecting to see her again. Now she was back in my life.

I invited her to Agua for a massage. I thought it was best to face this situation head on. The possibility of her blowing my cover lingered on my mind. In order to prevent this, I took special measure to make sure she was comfortable. We were led to a private room where two attractive men used their huge hands to knead our bodies into a state of rapture, before leaving us inflamed. Besides, we needed privacy for what we wanted to talk about.

We were both on our toned stomachs. We were lying upon separate massage tables in a room dipped in white. White curtains hung from the wall. Vanilla scented candles mixed with the scent of white tulips produced an enticing fragrance as we directed our eyes towards an open window, where South Beach was on exhibit. White towels covered our backsides.

"Still with the black," Natalie smiled, breaking the silence between us.

"What can I say, it's me."

Natalie hadn't changed much. She was still quizzical. One change I did notice…was her confidence. The person I remembered could barely look anyone in the eye. Now, she stared right through me.

"*Garcelle Jean Louis*. I never expected to see you again. Last time I heard, you were on the run. Now, you're all loved up with a baller," she spoke turning around on her side, resting her head on her right hand while exposing her buxom bosom. "Did the police decide to *just* stop looking for you?" She sneered sarcastically.

Rage filled my veins. My jaws began to tighten and my hands began to perspire. Though, I tried to act as if her statement hadn't affected me, but bad memories came back.

A year after my release, I got caught up in a murder investigation in Mississippi. That's why I relocated to Miami, hoping to escape my past. I wasn't a suspect in the murder; instead, the police wanted me to testify. And I couldn't hurt someone I cared about, even for revenge. But my past had still come back to visit me.

"I don't know what you are talking about. I know you aren't gonna take jail house talk for gospel." I tried to deflect her claims, knowing she could only have heard it through the grape vine.

"What do you want from me?" I asked in a hushed tone. She laughed. Knowing she had me in a bind, made her joyful.

"I want something just a little risky."

"I'm through with risk; I'm living a normal boring life." I yawned for effect.

"From what the Clarion Ledger printed, you enjoy risk and the man you chopped up did, too."

Inside I felt like exploding, the thought of making the newspaper had me uneasy. It meant that my mistake was on display for anyone to see. Since leaving the residential center, I'd killed over twenty men, most I didn't remember. But that assignment was different, because he was the one man I spared. His name was Thomas Willingham and he was the father of someone dear to me, someone I thought I loved. It was the one time I let my guard down.

Thomas was six feet tall, bald and black as night. He was a big player in the drug game. Even at sixty-five years of age, men quivered in his presence and that attracted me to him. The assignment to kill him turned into something else. I bestowed upon him my intimacy and he furnished me with explosive sex. His skills in bed were incomparable and he treated me like a lady. Instantly, he became the man that I'd dreamed about. I craved his touch and he craved what I provided. In turn, I fell in love. I couldn't finish the assignment and what was worse, my lover found out. What followed was something that I didn't want to relive…

"Why should I trust you?" I asked. A smile spread across her lips as she sat up straight, losing the rest of her towel.

"You can. We are cut from the same cloth. You let me in on your scheme and afterwards I'll be gone."

"How do you figure that I'm running a game?"

"The papers say you made away with nearly half a million." She got up and walked over to my table in all her naked glory. She ran her fingers across the edges of the table. "After I did some research on my own, I found three other crimes in different parts of the country with the same

M.O. I have to admit that you're getting better, because the police haven't gotten wise, but I have."

"You still haven't answered my question," I fumed. I wasn't going to let her string me alone.

What Natalie didn't realize was that I had changed a lot as well, from the time she knew me. I wasn't the same sheepish and loyal girl. Now, I took my destiny into my own hands. Killing men, for my financial security, was only a part of my persona. I wouldn't let anyone get in the way of my freedom. If Natalie wanted to try me, she would become another newspaper clipping.

"I need fifty grand." She commanded. "I have a situation."

"I guess you pissed off someone else."

Natalie was a former gambling addict. Obviously, that habit was hard to break. Addicts had a price; loyalty did not reside in them. They lived by a different code of ethics. Only a fool deals with addicts and for that reason alone, I would have to cut her off after she helped me accomplish my task.

"It doesn't matter. I need it and you need to stay free," she said with her fingers running across my arm. I pushed her hands away, turned around and sat up with my towel wrapped tightly around me.

The mystery man who contracted me for the Julian Steven's hit told me to do whatever I had to in order to get close to Julian. He needed a babysitter and with my record, no one in their right mind would hire me, so Natalie would come in handy. Natalie didn't have a record. She was court ordered in the mental institution, as a result of an emotional breakdown – following the loss of a large sum of money at a Las Vegas casino. For her assistance, fifty thousand was a small price to pay.

There was a knock at the door. Our time was up. One of the male masseuses stuck his head in.

"Is there anything else we can do? We need the room." He flirted, not knowing that there was much more that I needed, which only the stiff tongue of a man could provide.

"I just need one more minute, handsome," I coyly responded, while running my tongue across my lips. He winked and closed the door behind him. I returned my attention to Natalie.

"I'll see what I can do. If you want the money, you need to work for it." I ignored her, but could still feel the heat of her skin touching mine. "Is that all?" I asked, almost irritated.

Natalie got close to me, grabbed my towel, and unwrapped me like a gift. She then ran her finger up my thigh and stroked my wetness.

"There's just one more thing." She pushed me back down and pulled my waist towards her. I swallowed hard as nervous energy traveled through my body, causing goose bumps to rise on my skin. I felt like that young naïve girl back in Mississippi. I tried to push her away, to no avail. It wasn't that she was too strong. It was just that I needed to be touched. I was too weak.
"What are you doing?" I asked
"I'm working for it," she said.

   I admired my figure in the full-length mirror, dressed in a black negligee, complete with a sheer thong and corset. Not only was my outfit appealing, but it was easy to take off. Joull's last meal would be the envy of every man on death row. My hair was free flowing and my lips popped, due to my favorite *Mac* lip-gloss. I spritzed green apple body spray on my special place, knowing my forbidden fruit was worth eating.

   My skin was silky soft. I also took the liberty of getting my coochie waxed, leaving nothing but a strip for Joull to land on. The silhouette of my body danced on the pearl Venetian plastered walls as I swayed to the sounds of Miles Davis. The glow of candlelight was the only source of light, revealing bottles of massage oils and edible body paints on the nightstand. Using food during sex, made it more pleasurable, so I arranged a silver platter with slices of kiwi, mango and strawberries. I placed it atop the eight hundred thread count sheets that covered the bed. To make the evening even more festive, I decided to incorporate my favorite fruit, unpeeled bananas. He would know what to do with those.

This night would be the end of my assignment and like every assignment before, I made sure to catch my victims off guard and vulnerable. After I recreated his sexual fantasy, I'd end his life. My client gave me the word; thus, I was obliged to finish the job.

I hoped Joull didn't arrive before my surprise did. He enjoyed everything French; from his mansion built in the tradition of the French renaissance style, to his love of French food. I thought a ménage a trois would be enticing to his palate.

I walked across the marble floor out onto the terrace. I was greeted there by the smell of the ocean coming from the saltwater pool. I peered into the night sky and stared at the stars. They seemed close enough to touch and put me in a state of awe. It also put me in mind of a Mississippi night, where I discovered my love for darkness. Things were hidden in the darkness.

As I reached for the stars, I heard the hum of the Aston Martin's quad cam engine, as its tires screeched to a halt. He was home before I'd planned. His arrival made me nervous. I didn't expect him for another hour, at best. I gingerly walked down the winding stairway as the rustling of keys could be heard throughout the foyer of the expensive home.

Joull entered with a concerned expression on his usually jovial face. He barely noticed my outfit. I stretched out my arms for a hug just as I got to the bottom of the steps, but he didn't seem to care.

"I have no time," he said rushing past me towards the basement entrance.

There was something seriously wrong. I just knew that I couldn't let him go down into the basement, because my client ransacked it while searching for his money, money that was recovered, minus a hundred thousand. There was no way I could explain the state of his basement. I had to think quickly.

His hands were on the door as I stuck my tongue into his ear.

"Is that how you greet me?" I grabbed his hand and placed it on my behind. "I went through a lot to plan a surprise."

He squeezed me roughly. "You're beautiful." He mouthed while moving his hand down my thigh and turning to face me. His eyes surveyed my body.

He smelled like he'd been drinking hard liquor. The smell nearly turned me off. But I had to play the role; there was no way of overpowering him without catching him in a moment of weakness.

"If you think I'm beautiful, come upstairs with me," I noted, grabbing his hand. Surprisingly, he didn't budge.

"I have no time," he said, refocused on his task.

The kitchen was only a few feet away. I wondered how long it would take for me to retrieve a weapon before he discovered the basement. But there was no way that I'd make it before he flicked on the light switch. I was the only person who knew about his private retreat, the only person he gave access to it; therefore, I'd be the only one who faced retribution.

"I'm leaving." I threw up my hands as I walked away. "What happened? You're going back to your wife!" I yelled as I walked towards the kitchen.

Starting a fight was my only option. If he didn't take the bait, I didn't know what else to do. He came from behind and wrapped me in his arms. "She's not my wife and I'm not leaving you." He brought his point home by spinning me around and slipping his large tongue in my mouth.

"So prove it." I wanted to gag, but I held my composure.

"What can I do to make you happy, darling?"

"Just pay attention to me. All I ask for is your attention." I stared into his eyes looking for sympathy.

"Okay, okay." He started to kiss me again and tried to unhook my bra from the back.

He wore an electric blue suit. He wore a banana yellow shirt underneath his jacket. Still smelling of liquor, the stench of body odor filled my nostrils. In his country, deodorant wasn't a priority.

"No, no, no," I teased, shaking my head from side to side.

"Don't do me like this. I want sex now," he begged, discarding his jacket and lifting me in his arms and into the living room. He plopped down on an antique wing chair that could barely hold him.

"You have to take a bath Joull. I don't do dirty boys." I teased him after escaping from his large arms. I walked around the chair and wrote an imaginary heart on his baldhead. His olive skin glowed red as he blushed.

"Let me just touch you," he begged.

I lowered one of my bra straps, took out my breast, and showed it to him. "That's enough," I commanded. "You can do whatever you like after you have taken a bath."

Without saying another word, he rushed upstairs and into the master bathroom. The sound of water pelting the travertine tile brought a smile to my face and calmness to my soul. Men are simple. Show a little flesh and they become dumb. It's as if all the blood and brains rush to their lower head. My deception had led another bull to slaughter.

Still a little nervous, I retrieved my chronic stash and rolling papers from the bottom of one of Joull's priceless vases. After rolling a joint, I found solace through the back door. The sound of the three tiered water fountain provided calm. I took a seat on a chaise by the pool, hidden underneath the patio umbrella. I glanced at my watch.

Natalie was my surprise and she was running late. I didn't stress it, because other things occupied my mind, like getting into a zone before I dealt with Joull. Though killing him while he showered crossed my mind, it wouldn't accomplish the plan that I had in mind. Besides, I rarely killed in a sober state of mind. As I pulled from the joint, it helped me deal with my thoughts better. Being high helped bring things into perspective; it made a massacre an out-of-body experience, taking away the edge and heightening my senses.

Just as I entered a state of light-headedness, the sound of crackling dry grass caught my attention. Through glassy eyes, I saw Natalie heading towards me wearing only a black trench coat and fire engine red, four-inch stilettos. I recognized that there was something amiss about her demeanor. The smile that she greeted me with the other day was gone. She took a seat across from me and sat in silence.

"Garcelle, I can't do this." Natalie cried.

Her reaction surprised me. The promises she'd made during our encounter convinced me that she had it in her.

"You don't need the money," I responded, taking another hit. After exhaling a huge cloud of smoke, I continued. "We went over this yesterday. Why did you come here then?" I sighed, not needing another problem.

"I need the money. But it has to be a better way."

"There is no other way," I snapped.

"What did he do to me?"

"Shut the hell up. Your voice carries out here." I whispered looking around. "There's no going back, so if you can't do it, leave me."

She hesitated; I could see it in her eyes. She didn't want to leave, but she just didn't want to be an accomplice. There was no other way. She knew too much.

"There's a necklace at Harry Winston. If you help me get it, we can split it two ways," she pleaded. Natalie didn't understand that, for me, there was no going back. If I didn't carry out the assignment, I would take Joull's place and another price would be placed on my head. I needed to convince her to go into the house with me. My plan would fall apart without her.

"You love me, don't you?" I asked, appealing to her sensitive side. It worked with Joull, why not her.

"Yeah. I always have," she said tenderly, searching my face and catching my gaze.

Standing now, I strolled over to where she was sitting and slowly stroked her face. I held her chin in my hand, bent over, and placed a sweet kiss across her lips. She quivered, closed her eyes, and intertwined her tongue with mine. After a passionate kiss, I placed my finger on her lips. Taking her hand, I led her into the house and up the stairs into the master bedroom where Joull sat naked atop the bed with lust in his eyes.

I loosened the knot in the belt that held the trench coat tightly around Natalie's body, removing the coat from off each of her well-defined shoulders. The coat dropped to the floor and with my feet I moved it underneath me. Joull gasped for air as I got on my knees and licked a trail from the top of her foot, up her thighs. This was the first time that I'd gone there with a woman, but time was of the essence.

I directed Joull to lie on the bed as I gathered a bottle of strawberry flavored massage oil. "And you too," I said to Natalie. She did just as I had asked, which made me happy.

I tightened the handcuffs around his wrist, secured them to the bedpost, and covered his eyes with the mask. I rubbed him down with oil as I straddled the top of his huge stomach. Natalie crawled over to me in feline like fashion and I rubbed her down as well.

"I'm leaving her tomorrow. That witch can have everything. I love this, darling," he said, making empty promises.

"You sure," I said, as I massaged him with the warming liquid. He nodded his head in agreement while curling his toes.

"Cortez, said thanks." I sneered.

His eyes rolled in the back of his head as Natalie began kissing his neck. "Wha…," he responded, barely even hearing what I had said.

I put the tip of the blade on his chin, drawing blood. "Cortez said thanks." I smiled, running the sharp knife lightly across his neck. He froze, his eyes widened and he swallowed hard. I could feel his heart begin to beat quickly. His eyes searched for Natalie, but she was in the corner of the room, on the floor with her knees buried in her chest.

He was still confused. I read it in his eyes. "Who…What are you speaking?" He began to struggle, trying desperately to twist loose and to push me off, but to no avail. Like an expert butcher, I sliced into his throat and his words were replaced by a gurgling sound. As blood shot across the room, I could hear Natalie whimper. His warm blood trickled down my skin, covered my face, and I tasted it. I'd succeeded once more.

Joull was already gone when I got up from his bed. I walked over to Natalie and like a traumatized child she shook her head as I reached for her. She refused to take my hand. I walked by her, grabbed a towel, wiped the redness from my skin, and smiled at myself in the glass of the shower. Joull's pants were strewn on the floor. I dug in his pocket, removed money, a Cohiba, and his car keys. As I lit the Cohiba, I contemplated what to do with Natalie.

CHAPTER NINE

Julian

Andrea wasn't picking up her phone. I called, but I kept getting her voicemail. I wanted to apologize for the way I overreacted. There was no telling where the night could have ended or led. Even if we didn't have sex, the possibilities were endless. Desire lived between our kiss. Miko used to kiss me like that when our love was pristine and fresh. I wanted to experience that rush of heat that engulfed my body once more.

It was the first time I had taken off since bringing Aasia home from the hospital. I scheduled seventeen interviews for the Nanny position. Frederick was at the office taking care of the day-to-day operation. Thinking back on our encounter at the game, part of me wanted to apologize for doubting his work ethic. He was proving me wrong. After reading his figures for the next site, I was excited. If his investors came through, we'd be breaking grounds within months.

I looked at my princess for her approval as she buried herself deep in a notepad. She was every bit the carbon copy of Miko, possessing the same dark skin, almond shaped eyes and bright smile. Being tall for her age, modeling was possibly in her future. But the thought that she'd one day be a grown woman worried me.

"She's not nice. I don't like her," Aasia said, scribbling in her note pad with a crayon.

We were sitting in the living room interviewing an older woman; her stoic demeanor told me that she was unyielding, possibly the type that would abuse my daughter when I wasn't around. I could tell by the way she would flinch each time Aasia threw a tantrum.

Aasia was dressed in her favorite Princess costume that I'd bought her for Halloween. It was pink with a velvet bodice. She barely took it off, refusing to be seen without it, so instead of fighting with her, I let her wear it. Aasia's long, curly, black hair was pulled back into a lopsided bun, a reflection of a father's best attempt at styling. Trying to do her hair and keep her was still an event.

"Princess, who's gonna watch you when Daddy's not home." I stared at her, hoping she'd be sympathetic; though, I knew a four-year-old would only want what they wanted.

"Meeeeee!" She smiled, raising her notepad and crayon in the air in celebration.

"A grown up has to watch you," I said softly.

She threw her notepad to the floor, followed by her crayon, and slumped into the couch with her lips poking out in mock fury. I laughed and she smiled. Breaking out into laughter, we were lost in our own world, a world only me and my princess inhabited. We both forgot that we were interviewing a prospective nanny until she walked out without saying a word; then Aasia and I started to laugh again.

Aasia was exactly like Miko, impulsive and spontaneous. I never knew what to expect from her. She was only four years of age, but very intelligent. And the worst part was, she knew she had her father helplessly wrapped around her tiny fingers. Why not, she was all I had left.

My princess came into the world in the most devastating of conditions. Because of the quick thinking of the EMT's that arrived on the scene, life was brought out of the body of death. Looking back on the nights when I watched her battling to live, I feel joyful that she is healthy. In the hospital, many times I felt helpless and alone, not knowing what to do next, Miko's mother had a nervous breakdown after her only child's death, so I was left alone to raise my only child. All I could do was put my finger into her hands and show her love. That was what I was supposed to do. The doctors said babies that felt loved had a better survival rate. It was painful watching her struggle to breathe through the transparent plastic of the incubator. With each rise of her chest, I would exhale. I gave her my time then, because she needed me. She needed me to live. I just hoped I could focus on my business without losing her.

Children R Us was a reputable agency that provided nannies for some of the top executives around the country. I screened and selected ten nannies to interview from their agency, along with seven walk-ins from an ad I had placed. I scheduled only one more interview and was beginning to get nervous. Aasia didn't like the other nannies, either. I wanted her to feel comfortable, but if number seventeen didn't blow me away, one of the other women would just have to do. I glanced at my watch, hoping the agency's next nanny would be the one.

When she walked in one hour late, I was just about to tell her to leave, but she came bearing gifts. Holding a rather large, stuffed zebra, she instantly befriended Aasia with relative ease. Aasia ran in her direction with a huge smile on her face.

"The door was open. I hope it's alright that I just came in," she apologized as she entered.
"That's fine, but you know I need someone who's gonna be on time," I chastised, glancing at my watch as I stood up.

"I'm sorry. My name is Natalie Robinson," she said, extending her hand as Aasia tugged at the bottom of her pants. "I'm just inquiring about your nanny position."

"You're not from the agency?" I asked, puzzled.

She got on her knees, eyelevel with my daughter, distracting Aasia with the zebra while she loosened the barrette that held her lopsided do in place. Handing her a piece of chocolate, she took out a comb from the tattered leather bag that hung around her shoulder and ran it through Aasia's hair. I had the feeling that I had found the right person.

"What's your name, cutie?" she asked.

"Julian," I responded

She laughed and pointed at Aasia, "I mean the young lady."

"My name is Aasia," my daughter added. "My daddy's cute, too," she said, warming my heart.

Natalie directed her attention back to me. "No, I heard about the opening from a friend." She looked around. "I apologize. Were you expecting someone? I can come back," she wondered while gently taking care of my daughter's hair.

Natalie wasn't much to look at when I first met her. She wore no makeup and looked as if she'd just rolled out of bed. Her hair was in a bun and just as lopsided as Aasia's. Her clothes looked like they'd come directly off of the K-

Mart clearance rack. On her feet, she wore white sneakers that were scuffed and tied so tightly you couldn't see the tongue. The stone washed jeans she wore were something an old, white woman would wear. The jeans were buttoned inches above her waist and baggy, hiding any shape I doubt she maintained. But she seemed nurturing, someone I could trust to treat my child as her own.

"I like her, daddy. Can she stay?" Aasia asked, looking up at me with huge brown eyes. I couldn't resist. But I also had to make sure that Natalie wasn't a lunatic.

"Can I ask you some questions?" I smiled.

"Oh, I'm sorry. I'm so rude." She stood up, handing me a neatly typed resume detailing her work experience and education.

"No. *I'm* being rude. Can I offer you anything, maybe a cocktail?" I directed her to sit in a recliner directly across from the couch.

She declined the drink, which I liked. That told me she wasn't a slacker or better yet a drunk. I peered over her references; there weren't any lapses in employment. The fact that she watched a total of three children over a ten-year period was impressive. They were the children of some of the most powerful C.E.O's in the country, each going on to the best private school in their areas. Her techniques would definitely help Aasia.

"Tell me about your experiences. How would they help you in taking care of my daughter? She's not the most cooperative young lady sometimes."

Natalie crossed her legs and rubbed her chin in deep thought. Patience was a trait I found attractive in a person in authority and she exhibited it. She looked over at Aasia and Natalie's mocha skin took on a glowing effect. "Every little girl needs to know their place in a world. They need to know their worth." She stood, picked up Aasia, held my princess in her arms, wiped a smudge of chocolate from her cheek, smiled and stared into my daughter's eye with motherly compassion. "When I was a child, I never knew my worth. Not having a mother, I struggle with this to this day, but the children I take care of will never know what it's like when they don't have a mother, because that is what I'll be for them. I'll never desert her. She can always count on me."

Her words gave me chills. The fact that she came from the same family situation made me feel a lot better. I felt sorry for her hardships. But only she could know what another little girl could feel growing up motherless. Though, I never knew my mother, I had a father to guide me through boyhood. Now, Aasia would have a mother figure.

"You know about her mother?" I didn't remember telling the agency or anyone else that her mother had passed; if I did, it escaped my mind.

A rush of sadness passed over me. Since spending time with the neighbors, Aasia had been asking about Miko constantly. I couldn't let the truth escape my lips. The fact that her mother was dead wasn't something she could comprehend at her age. So I told her what my father told me about my mother. Miko was her guardian angel. Now I understood my father's madness. Maybe there was love in his heart after all.

Aasia warmed up to Natalie. She was sitting in her lap as happy as I'd ever seen her.

"When can you start?" I smiled in amazement.

"Right now."

"This isn't a regular eight hour gig. I'm very spontaneous. You may be needed overnight."

"I can handle it. I have no other obligations. Aasia will be my number one priority."

"You're hired." There was no doubt in my mind that I wouldn't regret my decision.

A part of me wanted to check her references before I hired her, but I didn't want her to walk out of my home never to see her again. The Valentine's Day event for Miami Noire's opening was the following week. I couldn't afford to take any time off to interview any other candidates. Besides, Aasia was in good hands.

My home office was serene, only the hum of the beverage cooler could be heard. I sat in a black leather executive chair, behind a writing desk with a marble stone top. With a pen in my hand, I stared at my business proposal underneath the white light spilling from my desk lamp.

It was nearly midnight when my phone rang; I had just put Aasia to bed and was working on a proposal for our next project. Another bank had rejected my loan request, making it nearly impossible to get the projected two hundred million dollar project off the ground.

When I answered, I was expecting someone else; maybe because I didn't expect to hear from her again.

"Hi," she said in a throaty voice. I didn't know what to say. I didn't know how to ask her about the other night.

"You decided to call. Who do I owe the pleasure?"

"I'm soooo embarrassed." She laughed.

"I think you conveyed that really well." I paused, set down the pen in my hand, and leaned back in my executive chair. "You could have at least told me that you made it home safely."

"That kiss…I haven't kissed anyone since Bryant." She paused, regret lived in her voice. "I felt like I was almost cheating. I didn't know if I could go there." Her voice grew heavy with emotion. "He was my first and only. I thought I could handle being touched by another man. But…"

I sighed, understanding her pain. Though I cheated on my wife while she was alive, sometimes I felt like I was being unfaithful every time I looked at another woman with lust. I still felt Miko's presence and guilt weighed down my heart. Because for me, every time I slept with another woman, it was like a slap in her face.

"Trust me, I understand. Maybe it's going to take you more time."

"That's just it. I can't continue living like this. I need to get out there and live. Bryant would want me to be happy."

"I thought you were *living*," I mocked.

"Maybe we both need to live a little."

"What does that mean? You won't walk out on me again and leave me looking like a fool."

"Are you asking me out?" I imagined her smiling on the other end.

"Yes." I cleared my throat, "That's if you aren't too busy at work or found something better to do.

"Let me know the time and the place." She paused. "But be prepared. I might not be in such a rush this time," she flirted. I smiled, hoping she wouldn't leave. If only for one night…

CHAPTER TEN

Widow

Blue was a cozy bar on South Beach, right off the main strip. It was the type of spot that allowed the anonymous to remain unseen behind the tinted glass of the storefront windows. As the seductive mix of house and experimental played, I found solace in a seat at the bar. Placing my black Jimmy Choo, studded hobo bag in my lap, I surveyed the crowd for my client. My attire was more fitting for the bedroom than a club packed with sex crazed men. I wore a black skirt by *Nanette Lepore* with a high front slit, a black, crystal-trim, v neck top that showed off my bust, and a pair of black, Dior, pointed-toe sling backs.

Old memories rushed back as I sipped on an *Incredible Hulk* while watching everyone enjoy themselves. This was one of my old haunts; I found it after leaving my life in Mississippi. It became my oasis during a time in my life when I acquired a taste for one-night stands, giving away for free what men died for, literally. It was one of the reasons I chose this spot to meet my next client. I needed to get laid. I could barely remember the last time a man had really put it on me, thug style.

Glancing at my Movado, I let out a sigh. I hated being stood up, especially when it came to business. I usually didn't meet my clients, but it was sometimes better to have a face to go with the name. There would be no names exchanged, but if I got screwed, I'd then know whom to look for. Besides, we hadn't talked numbers. I had put in all the work by gaining access to Julian's life. In my profession, it took time and money to set up a hit. But I preferred doing all the footwork. At least, it would be done right and that was why I demanded top dollar.

When he approached, I didn't know what to say. The face didn't fit the voice. The voice I remembered was masculine, He seemed a little feminine as he shuffled across the bar wearing a tight fitting white t-shirt, tight black jeans, and a red fedora set to the side. The red fedora was the sign that he was in the bar. He had a pretty face, prettier than some women. His long eyelashes brought out his piercing green eyes and his lips were glazed over with lip-gloss. After seeing his face, I couldn't help but wonder why he looked so familiar.

He gave off a cockiness usually reserved for the influential. Taking a seat beside me, he passed a manila envelop across the table. I held the envelope and realized that it was too light to be carrying cash.

"What do I need this for?" I asked holding the envelope in the air before letting it drop to the bar.

I didn't particularly care for him. That was my first impression. Maybe it was the way he stared at me, his glare made feel small and insignificant. It was as if he had already judged me to be less than he was.

He leaned forward in the chair, tapped his feet against the floor, and surveyed my expression. Contempt was written on his face.

"Just make sure Julian gets it. It's none of your concern what's inside."

"Anything I have in my possession is my concern," I fired back.

He waved the bartender over, ordered cranberry juice and Grey Goose vodka. After a few sips on his drink, he removed a cigarette from his shirt pocket, lit it, and let it dangle out the side of his mouth. He glared at me once more; the thought of being questioned by a woman bothered him. Lifting his glass and snatching the napkin from underneath, he took a pen from his pocket and scribbled on the damp napkin before passing it in my direction.

"Is that a good enough number to do as you're told?"

Though I didn't care for him, the number on the napkin wet my appetite. I crossed my legs, took the cigarette out of his mouth, to his astonishment, and took a pull. It was a bad habit I quit years ago, but murder made me want to smoke.

"Don't promise me something you can't deliver," I stated after removing the cigarette from my lips. He laughed. Like most men, he enjoyed aggression. It made him wonder if I was just as aggressive in bed.

"That's pennies. I just need you to deliver."

"I've done the hard part. I'm in his life. Just tell me when to finish him," I said, taking another pull from the cigarette.

"In due time, in due time… It can't be done until I feel comfortable that it won't come back to me. It's best for the both of us. I would hate to see your beautiful face behind bars." He rubbed my chin, making his point clear.

One thing that never surprised me about men was the fact that they could look down on you and still muster the strength to try to get between your legs. That sort of desire remained in his eyes as he checked me out, admiring the high slit in my dress and low cut of my blouse. But unfortunately, I didn't do pretty boys.

"And how do I know I can trust you to keep your word?" I asked, folding up the manila envelope and putting it in my bag to his satisfaction.

"Is this the face of someone you can't trust?" He smiled.

"Now I know I can't trust you," I said, rolling my eyes and putting the cigarette out in my drink.

"Don't be like that," he said, running his fingers through my hair. "Unlike most men, I keep my word."

I could barely stand to look at him, so I didn't. Instead, I stared past him and found a brother wearing an oversized red Yankee cap over his dreads. We locked stares; by the way he bit down on his bottom lip, I could tell he was undressing me with his eyes. The woman sitting across from him appeared to be his lover; she massaged his hands while his attention resided with me. It didn't matter to me whether or not he was taken. I wanted him and decided then that he would be mine for the night. She could have him back in the morning.

"I have one suggestion." I hesitantly took my eyes off the fine specimen of a man and returned them to my client.

"What's that, sexy?" He smiled, trying to find where the slit of my skirt led.

"Let's keep this businesslike." I looked him directly in the eye, 'I don't sleep with clients."

"Sleeping would be a waste."

I was sure he could charm the panties off a weak-minded type, someone that needed his type of attention. But what he didn't understand was that his words didn't mean anything to me. I've heard them all before, spoken by the best.

I yawned, letting him know how disinterested I was. "Like I said, I don't mix business with pleasure. Just do your part and I'd do mine. Once it's over, you go your way and I'll go mine," I said, standing up and retrieving my purse from the bar. Our conversation was done.

He grabbed my arm as I started to walk away. Tightening his hand around my wrist, he looked me in eye with a deadly stare. "Don't screw this one up. Falling in love isn't part of the job. Remember, keep it business and everything will fall in place. This can't come back to me."

He released his grip, stood up, paid for both drinks, and disappeared into the crowd. I couldn't explain it, but his man-handling of me had set me on fire. I enjoyed aggression and loved pain. I loved to have my hair pulled, my behind slapped, and to be choked during sex. Often, I wondered if it was a by-product of my rape.

The club was hot and smoky; I needed to get fresh air. It was cool when I got outside the club where a line of people waited for entrance. At first, I wasn't sure if my nipples were erect due to the cold air or because of what I was feeling inside. After wasting two months on Joull's minuteman sessions, I craved a real man.

When I saw *him,* I wanted to get his attention. It was Dreadlocks, the brother who eyed me in the club. He stood alone, next to a Black Cadillac Escalade sitting on twenty-inch chrome rims. The studded belt that barely held up his sagging skinny jeans sparkled underneath the dark sky. The wife beater he wore displayed tattoos that covered his muscular arms.

I sashayed in his line of sight, fully knowing that he'd speak.

"Shawty, what up?" he yelled.

I wasn't a groupie, so I kept walking as if I had something better to do. My arrogance didn't faze him as he walked cautiously behind. "I'm trying to know what your name is." He continued, finally catching up to me as I waited for the traffic light to change at the corner of Washington St.

"What's your name?"

"What's your girl's name?" I snapped back.

"No, Ma you got it all wrong. She's just a business associate," he claimed.

His voice got me even hotter. I could tell he was a New Yorker, because he had that east coast swag.

"Well, your associate or whatever you want to call her probably wouldn't appreciate you speaking to me." The light turned red and as the cars stopped in their tracks, I began to walk away.

"Let me spit something to you." He grabbed me by the elbow, increasing the steady flame that burned inside of me.

I let him lead me to his car where he leaned back on the hood with his hands on my waist.

"You better start spitting before your associate gets out here," I warned, admiring the earring pierced into his bottom lip.

"I'm trying to vibe wit you, shawty." He stared into my eyes, licking his luscious lips in the process.

"We can't vibe somewhere else?" I eyed him, while my hand rested on his pecs.

"Like where, I ain't from around here."

"Where you from?" I asked as if I didn't know.

"Straight from Harlem, fam. I'm here on business," he alluded.

The business he most likely was speaking of possibly had to do with drugs. I'd grown up around his type, knew that brothers like him moved from state to state in search of paper. If he knew what I knew, he'd quit. Most brothers either ended up dead, in jail, or on the wrong side of my blade.

I went into his pocket, found his car keys and said," I'll drive."

"Nah, ma I can't leave my boys."

"Are your boys gonna get you off tonight?"

We found ourselves behind a supermarket parking lot going at it like animals. His hands roamed between the fabric of my skirt while he kissed my chest in the passenger side seat of his SUV. I adjusted the seat back while grinding on him, sending us flying back. I removed my shirt, bra and skirt.

"Damn ma. You're wild," he moaned while touching my behind.

Turning around and discarding my panties in the back seat, I removed the plug from the cigarette lighter in his dashboard. It glowed red as I handed it to him.

"You want to get high?" he asked.

"Nah, I want you to burn me."

"What?" he asked, confused.

I leaned on the dashboard wrapped my hair in a bun, and moved it to the side. "Burn me while you hit it."

CHAPTER ELEVEN

Julian

Valentines day was a day I had battled with for three years. It was the day of love, but also the fourth anniversary of Miko and my father's death. The three years prior, I would visit her tombstone at the Wood Lawn Cemetery in New York City, but this year was different. Miami Noire's opening had coincided with that dreaded day.

Valentine's Day brought nothing but heartbreak for me. Seeing couples hand in hand and in heated embraces stirred the anger and pain in my heart. The color of roses and heart shaped balloons had me seeing red literally and figuratively. If not for the free advertising offered by Mahogany magazine to host the opening, I would have never left my house.

The opening was a black tie event; that attracted the wealthy. Walking the red carpet with Andrea on my arm, as flash bulbs popped, motivated me to put on my best mask. The smile on my face was a far departure from what I felt inside. Although being with her made my evening bearable, the pain inside of my heart made it difficult to really appreciate her beauty.

She looked exquisite with her dark locks pulled back in an up do with tight rolled curls. She moved across the red carpet gracefully, dressed in a black one shouldered gown that fell over the black sequined peep toe pumps on her feet. She also carried a metallic clutch that set off her outfit. And I complemented her well in a simple Armani tuxedo.

The event was the talk of the town. Celebrities came to be seen, politicians came to mingle, and the rich came to schmooze. Miami Noire had become the epicenter of the inherently shallow. As we made our way to the entrance, the scene before my eyes was awe-inspiring.

Walking across the black and white checkered marble floor and looking up at the dramatic glass roof as a string quartet played in the hotel's eighteen-story atrium lobby, I was at peace. I could barely contain my pleasure, seeing my vision come to life once again. The museum piece artifacts gave the lobby an art gallery type of feel. The Koi pond and surrounding lush imported Japanese greenery was something to behold. Made from steel, reflective glass, and combined with elements of art deco architecture, the hotel was a diamond in the Miami skyline. Located on Ocean Drive of South Beach, surrounded by white sands and sapphire water, my dream had become reality.

As we walked into the Japanese sushi bar named *Miko,* I felt a chill. The dining room's minimalist white and red décor was Asian inspired and infused the hotel with life. Authentic Teppanyaki chefs were dressed in Kimonos. They thrilled the guests at the hibachi tables while performing tricks with spatulas. And low walls made of shoji gave the room a cozy ambiance.

There was an absolute pandemonium as I entered the doorway and stepped down into the sunken lounge where I escorted Andrea to our seats. Revelers applauded me as I held my hand up high acknowledging their whistles and well-wishes.

To my surprise, a tripled tiered cake was wheeled out, engulfed in flames with the Noire, Inc. logo engraved into the fondant frosting. I rose as Frederick waved me over to blow out the candles. Like a true friend and brother, he let me bask in the glory, by stepping aside as I gathered my breath and blew.

My reception gave me a natural high; I'd become the most important person in that room, if even for a few minutes. That alone made it all worth it. It made the long hours, doubts and sleepless nights all worth it. As I glanced at Andrea, I realized I was opening a new chapter in my life.

Dinner was titillating. We feasted on Kanpachi with truffle soy and washed it down with Sake made at an Oceanside brewery in Fuji. It was what I imagined the food would taste like at an authentic sushi restaurant in Japan.

I glanced at Andrea as she finished the last of the Sake. She had been a delightful date and I wanted her to know how much I appreciated her company once again.

"I thank you for coming here tonight," I said, placing my chopsticks down.

"I thank you for having me. Your work is unbelievable. I really can't believe this all came from your mind," she said, impressed.

"I'm glad you found it enjoyable. It comes natural. It's my passion."

"We all need to be passionate about something. I just wish it wasn't always work," she said, avoiding my stare.

Andrea probably didn't know what she wanted as much as I did. But loneliness has a way of eating at its captives. Sometimes the thought of it caused those to seek the companionship of those they normally found undesirable. The face of loneliness was more unattractive than the most repulsive person alive. That emotion has caused more unwanted relationships and children than a little. Jamie Foxx blamed it on the alcohol. I blamed it on loneliness.

She was silent in the limousine car on our drive to the event. It was as if something was on her mind. I noticed her staring out the window at nothing in particular. Her eyes weren't only looking through the glass, but looking at anything we passed during our drive.

"Are you having problems at work?" I was concerned. It took a lot for a woman of her stature to become rattled.

"Only doubts…I put so much into making partner that I lost my passion for the law."

"You seemed fine the last time we talked. Did something happen recently?" I wondered, moving my seat a little closer. She hesitated answering. Instead, she searched in her clutch for a compact mirror to reapply her lipstick.

As my attention resided with Andrea, I felt strong hands massaging my shoulder. It was Frederick, wanting to talk to me privately. There was someone he wanted me to meet. I didn't want to press Andrea for a response, so I excused myself. I worked the room as we made our way through the crowd, shaking hands with anyone that was anyone.

"This is a close friend of mine, T.J.," Frederick announced, pointing to a short, skinny, brown-skinned cat in a black single-breasted suit with a black newsboy cap over his lo crop haircut.

"My name is Julian. It's nice to meet you." We shook hands. His grip was tight and he wore an emotionless expression on his face, as if meeting me was no big deal to him.

"What's up, bruh? This spot is tight," he complimented.

Frederick wrapped his arm over T.J.'s shoulder. "This is one of the investors that I told you about."

"What is your line of business? Do you work for one of the brokerage firms?" I asked, waving over a waiter that was making his way across the room with glasses of champagne.

They both laughed. Frederick laughed a little harder. I must have missed the joke, because I didn't find my comment funny.

"Money's money. Does it matter where it comes from?" T.J. asked as his expression returned.

"What he means is that he's serious about investing," Frederick intervened.

Frederick had done a lot for me. I viewed him as an important part of my life. I didn't want to let him down again. I didn't want to be too cynical. That wasn't me. I believed in supporting brothers like T.J. That was why I started Noire, Inc. with Darren over four years ago. I wanted to give my kind a fighting chance in a world where we were judged to be less.

"No need to explain. Let's set a meeting. We can go over some details and see if we can work something out," I said apologetically with a peaceful smile.

"That's good, money," T.J. replied.

"As a matter of fact, let's do it next weekend. We can connect in Atlanta and show Julian why it would be wise for him to build in Chocolate City," Frederick replied as the waiter arrived and distributed each of us a glass of champagne.

"Atlanta wouldn't be a bad move," I agreed, taking a sip from the flute glass.

"Atlanta is the only move, bruh." T.J. shook my hand as two men the size of Shaq stood beside him with bulges in their jackets. "I gotta be out, but be ready next weekend for a little southern hospitality," T.J. continued as he fist bumped with Frederick and threw me a peace sign.

"So what do you think?" Frederick asked as T.J walked towards the exit.

"I think if it's meant to be, it's meant to be." Those were the only words I could utter, remembering the last time I felt this way. I had the same nervousness the first time I came to Miami with Darren. He introduced an element into my life that I had not known and it nearly destroyed everything in its path. Maybe I was being paranoid, but something just didn't feel right.

As the night wound down, Andrea wanted to take a walk on the beach. I thought it would be a great opportunity to talk about what was weighing heavily on her mind. She didn't seem as enthused after our conversation about her work. I knew holding in frustration would only do harm. I knew more about that than anyone. That was how my marriage suffered with Miko. I allowed my unhappiness with work to tear us apart.

A cool breeze from the ocean refreshed us while we walked barefoot across the white sand. My pants were rolled up to my knees and Andrea discarded her dress into the waiting limousine and changed into a pair of black sweat pants to go along with a white tank top.

It was a gorgeous night and staring at Andrea underneath the radiant celestial bodies made the night that much more beautiful.

"This has been your night," she reflected, hitting me across the arm with her fist. I was happy to see her feeling better.

"In a way…Everybody wasn't there for me," I responded modestly.

"You weren't feeling like the man up in there?" she said, staring at me like I was crazy, continuing, "You should at least be happy that you've accomplished so much. Most people will spend their entire lives without that type of treatment," she said matter of factly.

"Can I be honest about something?" I wondered. I felt close to her at that moment and wanted to express myself.

"Go ahead."

"You sure you won't hold it against me?" I stopped in my tracks, making sure she understood.

"I can't hold something against you that you haven't even said yet," she reminded.

I inhaled deeply. "My wife died on this day four years ago." I surveyed her face to gauge her emotion, but there was none.

"So that's why a sista couldn't get roses or even a box of chocolates?" she tried lightning the mood.

I moved closer to the shore, standing on wet sand looking up in the heavens hoping to soothe that empty place in my heart. That was why I didn't allow myself to fall in love. That empty space was a reminder of what I lost. Subconsciously, I treated women coldly, because I didn't want to feel the pain that came along with admitting love.

"You miss her a lot." Andrea stood beside me, rubbing the tips of my fingers as we appreciated the view. She continued, "I understand. I wish I didn't, but I understand."

"We went through our fair share of drama. She cheated on me first; then I retaliated and did the same. I bowed my head as a tear made its way to the corner of my eyes. "But I'd give anything to trade the pain that I'm feeling now, for the pain I felt then."

Andrea slipped her arm through mine and with a little force she pushed me in the opposite direction towards an area where the palm trees provided us with privacy. We sat in the sand underneath a palm tree that seemed to engulf us. Andrea sat down Indian style patting my lap as I let my legs stretch.

"I used to argue with my husband about not taking me for walks. It may seem small, but in my mind, it was a huge deal. I'm from Georgia, so I love nature and fresh air; yet Bryant was from Chicago, so his thoughts on nature was a far departure from mine. He didn't like walking. If he even heard a branch break from beneath his feet, he'd want to go back in the house. I thought he was the most inattentive husband in the world. He did everything for me, but I couldn't see past the walks. It made me feel like he couldn't give me his all, so I held on to that resentment and it eventually caused me to have an affair." She looked away, still holding on to the embarrassment she felt. I put my hand on hers for support and let her speak. She exhaled, closed her eyes and continued, "When Bryant found out about the affair, it crushed him. I had never seen a man cry so deeply. It crushed me, I wanted to commit suicide and to make it worse, he walked in on me doing things to a man that I had never done with him. He didn't deserve it, not for hating going on walks." She looked me in the eye, squeezed my thumb and perked up. "He forgave me. I don't know what possessed him to do it, but he forgave me. We started going on walks together and it brought us closer. We started talking about everything, no matter how irrelevant it seemed. Through those walks, I found out about the man I married. He became my best friend. On one particular night, I was ill. I had a bad case of the flu. By that time, he liked walking so much that he'd go walking alone. But that night, he went out for a walk and never came back. They found him…They found him…" She couldn't gather the strength to say any more.

We embraced. I felt the presence of her tears on my neck as her body convulsed with grief. She didn't have to go any further. I understood why she avoided speaking about her husband, because she felt responsible for his death. Guilt was a hard pill to swallow, whether it was justified or not.

"It's not your fault. It's not your fault," I sympathized.

We stayed in silence as her cries died out, replaced by the eclectic sounds of music blaring from the clubs that called South Beach home. I put my jacket over her well-toned bare shoulders. "I'm sorry. I've been a bad date." She laughed, dapping at the remnants of wet mascara running down her mocha skin.

"You've just seemed like something was bothering you. I was just concerned. But outside of that, I couldn't have asked for a more beautiful date." I put my arms around her, pulled her close and held her.

Digging her feet into the sand with her head pointed towards the earth, she said, "Have you ever had to do something that you didn't feel right about? Something you felt was wrong..."

We must have been in sync, because after meeting T.J., I asked myself that same question. During a course of a person's life, we fight to do what's right. But most times, doing right isn't profitable, especially in business. Thus, we strive for a middle ground, instead of doing out and out wrong. But a middle ground doesn't always exist. Even a murderer justifies his reasons for murder. At the same time, I wanted to keep it real with her.

"I fight with right and wrong all the time. That's been the story of my life. Sometimes, it's the only way," I said honestly. She sat up breaking my grip and removed a wisp of hair from her eyes.

"Do you really believe that you have to do wrong sometimes? Is doing wrong easy for you?" She studied my expression intensely.

It wasn't that wrong was easy for me. I had the option of choosing what I wanted to do. I defined who I was as a man. But doing the right thing is the road less traveled in a world of mostly shallow people. If I didn't look out for myself, no one else would.

"Are you judging me now?" I wanted to know where our conversation was beginning to lead us.

"If you felt what you said was right, you wouldn't have to explain yourself." She moved further away, crossing her arms.

"Let me rephrase what I said." I exhaled, rubbing the top of my head as I wondered how best to respond. "All I'm saying is that we have to play by the rules sometimes to get ahead. And that means doing the wrong thing from time to time." Something in her eyes told me that wasn't what she wanted to hear. But I learned that sugar coating the truth wasn't beneficial for anyone. Ignorance isn't bliss. It's just ignorance.

"I don't know sometimes. I can't operate with those sorts of rules. How can I trust you if you'd do wrong to get ahead?"

"I tell you what… I'll make sure I'm honest with you at all times. You must promise the same." We shook hands, agreeing to be truthful no matter the consequences. It was good to have someone I could trust.

I moved closer and I wrapped her in my arms. Once again, as she rested her head on my shoulder, she fought to keep her eyes open. It was getting late and we both were tired. Looking at my watch, I wondered if Natalie had become another casualty of Aasia. I looked down at Andrea's face; her eyes were closed and peace radiated across her face. In a sleepy voice, she said, "I would love that, as long as you are honest with me. I'll be real with you."

I kissed her on the forehead tenderly, not in a friendly sort of way, but with passion. I followed it with a kiss more passionate than the first, this time on her cheeks. Her eyes opened, I noticed the light brown color of her iris as the stars illuminated us. She returned the favor by kissing me passionately on the lips, letting her tongue dance seductively in my mouth. I savored her cinnamon taste. Our kissing became harder and hungrier with each passing moment. Before I knew it, the sand had become my pillow and she was on top of me.

I put my hand on her waist and forcefully moved her body against mine. Moans escaped our mouths as we lost ourselves in ecstasy.

She held my baldhead between her hands. Though her touch was soft, it became harder each time I stimulated her spot. Her chest was her spot.

"That feels good," she moaned as she pushed me lower.

She wanted more. Her desire took control and feelings of infidelity to her deceased husband were no longer an issue. I removed my bowtie and took my shirt off with such voracity that I popped a few buttons. She touched my chest, laying her slender hands flat against my skin.

I gazed down at her as my hands traveled down to her sweats, pulling at the elastic while watching for her approval. She nodded her head and I obliged by pulling her sweats along with her panties downward and admired her body.

As I pulled the sweats over her long legs, I appreciated the imperfections, like the jagged scar under her left knee and quarter-sized birthmark on her thigh. She quivered as I got on my knees and kissed around her belly button piercing, licking a trail from her belt line to her lips and back down again.

"You have protection?" She asked.

"No," I said, kissing her on her breast.

"We got...ta stop," she moaned as I continued. I thought she was talking nonsense because her body said yes.

I kissed tenderly along her torso, finally reaching her chest.

'No, we have to stop," she demanded, pushing me away. But I kept kissing on her chest stimulating her spot thinking that her resolve would weaken. But she was serious, shoving me stiffly in the chest.

"You sure?"

"Yeah. I can't do this."

My passion throbbed, but there would be no relief for that feeling. I got up and she gathered her clothes quickly. There was fear in her eyes and I wondered why. As consenting adults, we could indulge our passions without fear of retribution. We weren't married or committed to anyone; yet, she exhibited the appearance of a guilty woman. That troubled me, made me wonder if I could trust her.

She shook the sand from her hair and clothing, wiping between her legs and removing the grains of sand that stuck to her skin. I rounded up my clothing as well, wearing a look of frustration as I put them on my body. Once she was dressed, she began to walk away. I watched as she proceeded to the limousine like she had regretted what we had shared only moments earlier.

Then something came over me. It was the bitter pill of rejection. That emotion was something that I hadn't experienced since Miko.

It scared me, because I realized I had feelings for Andrea, feelings that possibly could be love.

I hadn't moved an inch, still staring as she disappeared into Miami Noire. After another minute, I swallowed my pride and followed behind as the long walk of humility numbed me. I contemplated what I was feeling, wondering if it was the beginnings of love or lust. Maybe it was my competitive spirit moving me, since I hadn't conquered her.

I walked underneath the stained glass skylight in the entrance court and across the granite entrance drive. The entrance drive was empty except for the black limousine I arrived in and another car whose high beams nearly blinded me as they unexpectedly turned on. With my hand shielding my eyes, I looked for the face of the offender.

The car's engine hummed. Its tires burned against the black pavement as it began to move. My heart stopped, I was frozen in place, couldn't move. Like a frightened animal, fear had paralyzed me. The tank of a car barely missed me. It was a rusted Cadillac El Dorado. Stopping in front of me, the windows went down slowly and I got a glimpse of the man inside. It was Carl wearing a red fedora with a cigarette dangling from his lips. He smirked at me as if my fear had excited him.

"Watch your back, because the next time you won't be so lucky." With his hands he made a cutting motion across his neck, then burned rubber as he drove off.

Fear lived in me. The fear of God lived in me.

CHAPTER TWELVE

Widow

I needed it. I needed it bad. It was nearly three in the morning when I left Julian and I needed to find a man. I needed someone to beat me up, pull my hair and get physical with me. I felt bad for not getting Dreadlocks' number the night he put it on me in his SUV. Hell, I didn't even know his real name. But names were the last thing on my mind.

I was an addict when it came to sex. My desires were too strong. I'd held them at bay for a while, but I was once again in search of that fix. That need had me strung out years ago. I'd relapsed, found myself turned on by a man's touch.

It felt good to sleep in my own bed, covered in my own three hundred-thread count seats, serenaded by the sounds of J Holiday. I lived in a breathtaking million-dollar ocean front condominium in the Residences at Gansevoort South, an upscale dwelling that overlooked the teeming Miami skyline and Biscayne Bay.

A pillow was clinched between my thighs. On occasion it helped me cope with that throbbing need. It prevented me from losing my mind, but at that moment, all it did was incite my wanting to the second power. I needed fresh air, a place where I could clear my head.

I found peace watching the stars. So I wrapped the sheets around my body and walked onto the balcony, ten floors above the ground. I had a fear of heights, but I felt safe behind the glass railings, which I held onto tightly.

I thought I would get peace at four o'clock in the morning, but I was wrong. Through the open floor to ceiling glass doors of the balcony directly across from me, I could hear a commotion. It sounded like a heated argument and only a lover's quarrel would cause such hostility at such a late hour.

At first, I was upset. I was angry that my peace was ruined. But it only lasted a second, before *he* came out on the balcony. I couldn't take my eyes off him as he held his package while taking a slow hit from a Newport cigarette. Dressed in only baggy blue jeans, sans a shirt, I noticed his shape .He had a jail house build. His toned physique could only be a product of killing time out in the prison yard.

Our balconies weren't close, but close enough that I got a good look of his masculine features. The look on his face told me that he had a lot on his mind. The lines in his forehead and the crease around his eyes also told me that he was stressed. We locked stares. He nodded and I waved slightly. I didn't want to be rude or too transparent. I decided to let him make the next move. There was nothing as impulsive as a frustrated man.

"Are you new around here?" he asked, blowing smoke into the breeze while walking to the end of balcony that was closest to mine.

"I should be asking you the same," I said.

"My name's Truth."

I smiled, to finally have gotten a name, even if it wasn't his real name and said, "I'm the Lie." I flirted, even though I was being truthful at the same time.

"That's cute, but what's really your name."

"Does it matter?" I asked.

His eyes ran over my body. I could tell he was interested by the way he bit his bottom lip. In my profession, I learned to read body language. His body language showed nervousness, the language of a man who felt guilty about what he was thinking. The lines in his forehead disappeared, replaced by arched eyebrows. He was curious.

Then *she* appeared. I wasn't sure if she'd come out to finish their argument or to search for the other voice she heard floating in the air. But she appeared, fully nude with fury spilling from her pores. She was a red bone, with blond hair,

surgically enhanced breasts, and a huge behind
that was probably augmented, as well.

"Who is this chick?" she yelled, pointing at me
with acrylic fingers.

"We just out here kicking it, go inside. You've
said enough for the night," he yelled, discarding
the remnants of his cigarette to the earth below.

"Who are you trick?" she asked me.

I didn't say anything. My head was pounding
from anxiety and I didn't need any more drama,
especially not just for talking to her man. I could
tell my silence infuriated her as she searched our
faces for answers.

She glared at me and then at him; then while
removing her hands from off her hips with wrath
in her eyes, she slapped him across the face. I
almost didn't know what to expect. I feared for
her life. She was an itty bitty little thing, not
more than five feet and looked like she didn't
weigh more than a hundred pounds soaking wet.
But still I expected him to do what most men
would do in the presence of a third party. Let it
slide and swallow his pride.

She tried hitting him once more, but this
time he caught her arm in mid swing and
wrapped his hands around her throat, lifting her
tiny feet from the ground, squeezing tightly
around her windpipe as he spoke.

"You ever touch my face like that again and I'll kill you. I don't care who's watching," he said directly into her ears.

She tried nodding her head. She could barely move as he tightened his grip. Her eyes bulged from its sockets, lined with tiny red veins. She couldn't breathe and from the corner of her eyes, she searched my face. She was possibly expecting me to run for help or at the very least be disgusted. But she didn't know me. The sight of his strength only increased my appetite. I wanted him even more.

"Don't ever question me again. I'll deal with you when I say I will." He released her, dropping her to the floor where she gathered her breath. He walked away, disappearing into the condo too angry to care about her welfare. After getting her second wind, she chased behind him. There was more arguing, which only intensified my headache. That was my sign to go to back to bed.

I left the balcony door open, allowed the cool air to chill the heat between my thighs as I set my alarm to make the best of my few hours of sleep. Crawling back into my bed, I once again put my pillow between my legs hoping that sleep would overtake me and usher me into a state of serenity.

I had finally discovered peace when I heard my doorbell. Searching for my alarm clock through blurry eyes, I was disappointed to find that I'd only slept a total of ten minutes. And I was even more peeved that I had to get up.

But slumber overtook me once more and I fell into its grasp. That was when the knocking began. The sound of fist hitting against imported wood rang throughout all two thousand square feet of my condo. This time I got up, sat on the edge of my bed to steady my throbbing head, and hoped it wasn't the girl from the balcony.

Walking across the imported marble, I could only hope that whoever it was had a good excuse. I looked at the CCTV monitor sitting on the granite countertop in my kitchen and saw Truth. His shirt was still off and he appeared anxious as he leaned on the front door listening for a sound.

I walked nonchalantly to the door, took my time unlocking each lock, and only opened it slightly enough that he got a good look at my face.

"Do you know the time?" I asked, hoping that he didn't expect to just to walk in.

"I thought we had a connection," he reasoned.

"What would have given you that idea? We barely talked. Besides, I don't wanna risk you getting pimp slapped again. So, good-bye." I tried closing the door, but he was stronger than me. Wedging his hand and Timberlands between the door, he stared me in the eye. "I saw the way you looked at me."

"Are you seeing the way that I'm looking at you now?" I glared at him, turning my eyes into slits. "How do you know I don't have a man in here?"

"Your sheets. That's how I know." He looked at my sheets, his eyes canvassing where my paradise was. For the first time, I noticed the white sheets were damp with my juices. "A real man would've taken care of that already." Pushing his way into my apartment, he pulled the sheets off my body.

I was speechless as his fingers traveled down the center of my sternum. All I could do was tremble at his touch. The door closed behind him. He put his hands on my waist and lifted me into the air with ease. I wrapped my legs around him, locking them around his glorious behind as he led me to a spot in my kitchen atop the granite countertops. The kitchen erupted with noise as he pushed aside pots, pans and silverware off the surface of the countertops and onto the marble floor below. I quivered as he sat my naked bottom on the cold granite. My headache gained momentum.

My moans were the soundtrack of our clash of desire. We didn't say a word to each other; there was no need to talk during lust. People only talked dirty to make up for their lack of skill. He didn't need to do that. I didn't need to do that for our bodies were in sync. Our temples complimented each other like two musicians who had never played together, yet their individual talents alone made that fact irrelevant.

He was Branford Marsalis; I was Angelique Kidjo singing a melody as he blew on my sexophone. My sexophone was my breast, each nipple was a mouthpiece and the vertebrae of my spine were the tone holes where Truth composed his music. He was the best sexophonist I had ever had, yet he didn't know whom he was dealing with.

I was trouble, and men that got involved with me found that out the hard way. If Truth thought this was going to be more than it was, then he was wrong. He wasn't an assignment, so he'd only have me once. I'd make it an enjoyable time, but he knew where I lived so the rules strictly applied.

He grinded roughly against me and was at the brink of ecstasy when I stood up and left the kitchen, leaving him frustrated. I walked through my bedroom and onto the balcony and stood there naked with my behind pressed against the glass railing. He followed behind me like a good doggy with confusion in his dark brown eyes.

"What are you doing, Ma?" he asked, standing by the sliding door afraid to cross the threshold.

"If you want it, you got to come out here for it."

"You're bugging. Nah, get your pretty little dump in here, so I can wax it."

"Are you deaf?"

"No, but my wife…," he whined. I didn't like whiners. If he kept it up, the only place he'd get it would be between his hands.

"I understand…you're scared," I teased.

He put his foot over the threshold cautiously, looked over at his balcony and backed up again into my bedroom and said. "I'm out… this is crazy." He gave me his back and began to walk out of my bedroom.

I didn't move. I knew he wasn't going anywhere. And within seconds, he proved me right when he came back. His desire had no conscience, unlike that little heart of his. He cautiously walked across the threshold and looked at his balcony once again, but she was nowhere in sight; though the sliding glass door to his apartment was still cracked open. But this time, he kept his pace and began to kiss me as soon as we touched. He tried forcing himself inside of me. But I wouldn't let him.

"Come on, Ma. Why are you trying to play me?"

"I'm not playing you. I just want it to be dangerous."

He looked frustrated. "Like how? Isn't this dangerous enough for you?" he asked, pointing towards his balcony.

"Nah, not dangerous enough."

"So how do you want it?" He whispered with angst in his voice.

"Put me on the railing," I commanded. He lifted me up onto the railing, his hands tightly around my waist. "Almost there."

"What else could you possibly want?"

"Choke me. Put your hand around my neck and choke me while you're sexing me."

"You're serious."

I gave him the eye and he put his hand around my throat as he entered me. I was in heaven. There was nothing more orgasmic than danger. I moaned loudly, hoping to arouse his wife's suspicions as he held onto my throat. The fact that I could fall to my death if he lost concentration aroused me, as well. And as my neck went numb, the prospect of dying in his hands excited me even more.

CHAPTER THIRTEEN

Julian

It was a gorgeous day. The sun beamed from the heavens into my kitchen, giving it an incandescent glow. Fresh air seeped through the open casement windows, providing the kitchen with a wild jasmine scent. The blue Herron sung harmoniously with the morning doves.

"How was she yesterday?" I asked Natalie as she sat down at the kitchen table. Aasia was still sleeping, so I invited her to eat breakfast with me. "Be truthful. You look tired as hell," I said noticing the bags underneath her eyes.

My personal chef had cooked breakfast and we were enjoying all the staples of a southern style morning. He prepared buttermilk biscuits, grits, pork sausage, and scrambled eggs. I needed to eat something before I chartered a private jet and headed to Atlanta to meet Frederick and T.J.

"I just ran two miles. That's why I look beat, gotta lose this baby fat" She patted her toned mid section as her face glistened with fresh droplets of perspiration. "Actually, Aasia and I had a great time," she reminisced as a smile crossed her face.

I was happy to see that things were working fine. Aasia was becoming better behaved and seemed to enjoy her time with

Natalie. Whenever I got home, she was tucked into bed and had been on a consistent schedule. Natalie treated her like her own and that warmed my heart.

"What did you two do?" I asked wondering what caused the glow on her face.

"I threw a little birthday party for her. I had a few of her friends come over and we had some cake and played games."

"You didn't ask for my permission," I snapped.

"I didn't think you'd mind. Besides, her birthday was last week and you hadn't done anything for it," she said.

I didn't want to wake Aasia, so I let it go for the moment and simmered in private. There was a reason behind why I never celebrated my daughter's birthday. Because of what had taken place on the day she was brought into the world, I thought it was best to keep it from her until I knew how to better deal with it. My intent wasn't to deprive her, but whenever her birthday came I was in too bad a shape to even think about celebrating. Natalie wouldn't understand that reason. Most people couldn't understand.

"Just let me know next time you do something like that," I directed.

I didn't mean to be a stickler. But I wasn't in the best mood. Andrea was missing in action, again. I played the bug a boo role and called her about three times a day, but she didn't return my calls. I didn't understand her. It seemed like anytime we got physical, she'd go into hiding. I didn't like that about her and I was beginning to think that maybe she had someone else.

We ate in silence. The sound of silver clashing against stoneware had become the only signs of life. Natalie ate her food like a man. She didn't waste getting her grub on with all the necessities required by most women and that in of itself was a turn on. It was a sign that she was uninhibited in the bedroom.

"Oh, something else slipped my mind. This was laying on the front steps," she said, handing me a manila envelope from her bag.

I surveyed the envelope. There wasn't a return address or any postage affixed to it. The envelope only had my name written across the top.

"This was on the front steps?" I wondered, a little bothered that it didn't have my address.

"Yeah, it's probably from one of the neighbors," Natalie reasoned.

I put the envelope in my briefcase, turned on the flat screen television tucked underneath the custom maple cabinets, and turned it on high. There was a news report about a fire that destroyed a home in Key Largo about a week earlier, which wasn't too far from my home. The reporter said the fire marshal found a body in the blaze. After conducting an autopsy, the victim appeared to have been killed prior to the fire. They had no leads and were still conducting a full investigation. It was my first time hearing about the fire and it unsettled me, because I worried about Aasia's welfare whenever I wasn't around. It seemed that no matter how beautiful and safe a place seemed to be, there was always the possibility of tragedy.

"I can't believe all the sick people out on the loose," Natalie said, watching the reporter interview the shocked residents of Key Largo.

"That's the world we live in." I took a sip of my coffee and glanced at my watch. The meeting was very important, since my last proposal was rejected. It had jumped to the top of my priority list. I had to be wise with how I allocated money for my next project. With the economy in flux, I couldn't use all of the company's available funds for such a project without putting our future at risk. So it was a possibility I'd have to go the untraditional route.

"You say that like it's okay," Natalie said, jumping back onto the subject.

"I'm not saying it's okay, but it's a part of life. We can't do anything to change it," I said, alluding to the fact that we as humans are helpless against the atrocities that plague our society. I dropped my fork and leaned back in my seat.

"Anything can be changed. Anyone can be changed."

"I won't say it's not possible, but I've never seen it." I said, loosening my belt and rubbing my stomach.

What I liked about Natalie was that she had her own opinions and didn't hesitate to express them. Talking about world events had become our normal routine in the morning before I departed for work. Our playful debate had become the highlight of my days.

She stood up, collected the plates, emptied the contents into the garbage disposal, and washed them by hand. As she stood over the double sinks, I got a good glimpse of her burgeoning shape. Tight spandex style Capri's contoured quite exquisitely around her rotund derriere and her firm breasts were well supported in a gray sports bra. Up until that moment, I hadn't noticed how attractive she was. But she had snuck up on me. It was like witnessing the release of a beautiful butterfly from its cocoon.

I couldn't help but envision how she'd look totally nude. The sweat that stained the fabric between her thighs had me on edge. The perspiration that covered the fine hairs on her toned back made me think of hot passionate love making. And her strong calves were that of a champion jockey who had ridden her fair share of stallions.

I began to lust after Natalie. Maybe it was because I hadn't had sex in some time or because I was truly into her. Since meeting Andrea, I craved for something more than just a simple roll in the sack. I wanted a meaningful relationship. Andrea had turned on that switch in me, a switch that propelled me to covet a woman's total sexual surrender.

The gentle throttle of the dual Cessna engine nearly put me to sleep as I lay back in plush light gray leather seats thirty thousand miles in the sky, reading the latest issue of Mahogany magazine with me on the cover. It hadn't even hit newsstands, yet and there I was dressed in a navy blue pinstriped suit with a globe in my palm, looking like I had the whole world in my hands. Too bad it was the furthest thing from the truth. I barely had a handle on own my life. There was no way I could help anyone else.

My surroundings were splendid. The cherry wood foldout executive table held my reading materials. And the shine of the brushed gold complemented the Australian walnut woodwork to perfection. As I looked at the empty seat beside me, my mood immediately went sour, because no matter how ornate the surroundings, I was still alone.

But I let work occupy my mind like usual. I opened my brief case to look at the projected figures for Noire, Inc. for the next quarter and stumbled across the manila envelope Natalie had found earlier. I broke the seal and noticed what looked like photographs inside. There was also a letter inside and it too had my name across.

Dear Mr. Stevens,

You ruined my life and the lives of my family, including my children. Did you ever think of them before you accused me of something that I hadn't done? I was a loyal and trusted confidant of Darren Edmonds for ten years and filled the same role at Noire, Inc. for the last four years.

Throughout my employment, my records were flawless. There was never a discrepancy on my watch. Did you think of that before you decided to play god and destroy my life as well as my reputation?

I've lost my home and my only means of supporting my family. My son suffers from acute leukemia and thanks to you, we can't afford his treatments.

I bet you think you have won. I bet you think you're going to have me sent to jail. But you're wrong. I will spare no expense when it comes to

getting my revenge. You will beg me for mercy by the time I'm done with you.
Sincerely
Your worst nightmare
P.S* Make sure you have two million dollars if you want to keep our secret, secret. You have twenty four hours. You know where to meet me.

As I took out the other contents of the envelope, my heart felt like it had stopped in mid beat, lightheadedness then set in, followed by a cold sweat. I couldn't believe my sight. I closed my eyes, rubbed my hands against my eyelids and opened them slowly. But the photographs were still there as well as the images they contained.

The photographs were of Simone and I. She was one of Darren's call girls that I'd become quite smitten with. I barely remembered that night in Miami. I only remembered waking up covered in blood. I never thought I actually killed her. I always believed that Darren was involved in some way.

But the photos told what I couldn't remember. In one picture, I was covered in blood and my hands were wrapped tightly around a rope that was wrapped tightly around Simone's neck. We were both naked. She was on her knees and I had entered her from behind. Ecstasy was written on my face and pain was written on hers as she tried prying the braided rope away from her neck with bloody hands.

There was another picture of us but Simone was no longer fighting. She lay limply on the crimson stained sheets as I continued sexing her from behind. There was no longer life in her body, the wide eyes stare was the same wide-eyed stare Miko displayed the day she died. I couldn't contain my tears, couldn't stop the salty beads from flowing down into my mouth. And worse of all, I could hear Darren laughing at me from the grave.

When I arrived at Atlanta Hartsfield airport, my mind was in a different place. After seeing those photos, I feared for my life, as well as my future. I also thought about the two-million dollar asking price for Carl's secrecy. I didn't have that type of money at my disposal. Though I lived well, I also invested heavily in Noire,Inc. and survived on a modest six-figure salary. There was no way I could liquidate my assets quick enough to pay him, nor did I want to.

A chauffeured Rolls Royce Phantom whisked me to the Buckhead section of Atlanta where T.J owned a gentlemen's club named *The Spot*. As soon as I entered the establishment and was led up to the V.I.P lounge, I understood exactly where the club got its name. Beautiful chocolate women entertained at each corner of the club displaying their flawless Brazilian waxes to throngs of sex-crazed men.

Business was important to me. Focus was important, as well. A gentlemen's club was in direct opposition to what I held in high esteem. It wasn't a place to discuss business. It was a place to unwind and relax. And at that moment, they were the last two things I wasn't capable of doing.

A cloud of Marijuana smoke seeped out of the V.I.P room as soon as security opened the door. The music blasted at astronomical decibels as a group of men enjoyed the entertainment of a room filled with women. Tiger print carpet conveyed the animalistic desires that were on display as the women danced in various states of undress. Black leather L shaped sectionals became the stage where the dancers gave one on one attention, while others danced for an audience on a stage in the corner of the room. Free drinks flowed in excess from the private bar. And dim lighting provided the room with a seductive ambiance while concealing the shameless acts of a few inebriated men. All combined to turn the room into a hotbed for pure unadulterated yearning.

This wasn't my scene, though it once was. I vividly remembered the first time I was thrown into the same sort of revelry. It fascinated me then, but now I wanted no parts of it, because I knew where it could lead. And because of my introduction to such debauchery, blood was on my hand.

Frederick sat in the middle of the room in a captain's chair in the mist of a lap dance as he smoked on a flawlessly rolled Cohiba filled with Atlanta's finest. The dancer that captivated his attention was almost surgical in her approach. She had perfected the movements of a sex goddess. I watched her, the way she crouched over him with her back to his face while gliding her amble behind along his lap, without losing footing. Phenomenal was the only way to describe her precise movements. Her caramel skin, long blond hair and slanted eyes enslaved my total attention. I could not look away.

"You like what you see?" a voice said from behind.

"Is it that obvious?" I asked turning around and coming face to face with T.J. He wore white-framed Prada wrap glasses, black jeans and a green Coogi shirt.

"Nasty usually has that affect on men," he laughed. "Do you want to have a private dance after old boy is done?"

Nasty was a very unusual name, especially for someone so stunning. Still I was curious as to how she got her name.

"All I want to do is talk business," I said, wanting to get to the core of why I had even come to Atlanta.

"I conduct business better when I'm relaxed. Boardroom meetings bore me. I'm not the sitting down type."

"I'm the total opposite. But I do believe there's a time and place for everything and this is neither the place nor time to discuss business," I stated, looking around the venue. I wanted to leave, I felt disrespected by the unprofessional manner in which they were handling business.

T.J's jaws tightened. He motioned for the D.J to kill the music, snapping his fingers, though the music drowned out his attempts. The music continued and I could sense it angered him. He walked to where the D.J. was mixing his CD's and confronted him. With a swift backhand slap to the D.J.'s face, the music abruptly stopped, but his assault did not.

The man cowered as T.J rained down blows on him. Fear was etched on the faces of all onlookers and I got the sense that it wasn't the first time that T.J had displayed that type of fury. And it wouldn't be the last.

After security cleared the room and escorted the bloodied D.J. out the club, T.J. and I sat across from each other as the burning fireplace provided us with warmth. Like usual, Frederick opted to fulfill his desires as he took Nasty into a private room for a private dance and possibly more.

Considering that he had viciously battered a man for not hearing him in a noisy room, I got the feeling that T.J wasn't forgiving or sympathetic. I even wondered if there was a heart inside of him. I came from the street and understood that men like T.J knew only one way of gaining respect. In his mind, the only justice was street justice.

"You have a way of getting your point across," I said sarcastically, wanting him to know his tactics hadn't shaken me.

"Compared to what I got growing up, Ole boy got it easy," he remarked, waving over an overly attentive bartender from the private bar. "Have a drink. It'll make me comfortable."

The bartender rushed to our sides, his eyes nervously scanning our movements. I felt for him

"I'll have a gin and tonic," I offered.

"I want the usual and make it quick," T.J. snapped, without the slightest hint of remorse.

The bartender's hand shook as he filled my glass. He too was fearful of doing something to provoke T.J.

"I have to be honest with you. I don't like the way you conduct business," I said as two ice cubes were dropped into my drink.

The bartender placed a bottle Hennessey in front of T.J. and disappeared into the club. "Fear is the international language. If they fear you, they won't cross you," he said, taking the bottle to the head.

He reminded me of Darren and that caused me anxiety. They were cut from the same cloth. In his warped mind, intimidation was the only means of communication and pleasantness was a sign of weakness. They were men who prided themselves in being bloodthirsty. At the same time not taking into account that men who lived by those rules, usually died by them.

I looked around the club, took in the mosaic tiles that lined the walls and the top-of-the- line flat screen televisions above the cherry wood bar and I wondered what T.J. needed me for.

"Why get into the hotel business? You appear to be doing well for yourself." I leaned back and crossed my legs, while studying his stoic demeanor for any cracks.

"Ever hear of the Roads of Buckhead?" he asked.

I knew of it, because it was one of the biggest projects in development in all of Atlanta. It would become home to some of the foremost boutiques, restaurants and world-class high-rise residences in the United States. Its address alone would catapult any company associated with it into world-renowned status.

"Yeah, I'm aware of it."

"My uncle owned Ellis Construction and was a re-developing and construction partner of the Roads of Buckhead." His face lit up. "They are looking to add an upscale boutique hotel to the mix. I thought we could make that happen."

The prospect of opening the next Noire in Buckhead instantly brightened my disposition. It would provide exactly the type of splash that I wanted for my next location.

"Where do you come in at?"

"My uncle passed last month and I inherited his majority stake of the company." He gazed off into the distance, showing the first remnants of emotion.

"I'm sorry to hear about your loss," I said consolingly.

"From what I hear, you aren't a stranger to loss. I'd like to offer my condolences for your wife and father."

I bowed my head, looked into my glass, and wished for the moment to pass. Anytime anyone offered his or her condolences, I felt a sense of failure. Anyone with intimate knowledge of my situation knew what had transpired and that made me feel less of a man. And in those moments, I exuded fragility.

"I appreciate it."

"I know how you feel."

"Maybe to a degree…" There was no way he could know my pain. Possibly he knew the pain of losing a loved one, but not the pain and inadequacy that I lived with on a daily basis.

"No. I know how you feel." He threw his head back and took another long swig of that pain-numbing potion.

I wanted to change the subject. I didn't want to dwell on the past.

"Getting back to business…What are the specifics?"

"It's simple. I've already acquired six acres of land that we can use for the site. And it's already developed."

I still didn't understand where Noire, Inc. shined in all of this. He didn't need us and I could see it and I knew he did. There had to be more to his interest.

"Why us? Why do you need us?" I wondered, twirling the watered down liquor around the glass.

"Frederick told me that you were having cash flow problems. You're looking for investors?"

"Yes, we do need investors. You seem like you could develop a hotel of your own."

"True. I have the resources and the cash, but I don't have a recognizable name. Noire is hot right now and the Roads of Buckhead only wants what's hot."

"How much are you willing to invest?" I doubted anything he wanted to invest would put a dent in the one hundred million needed to complete the project.

"I'm willing to invest seventy five million," he said proudly.

His gentlemen's club was one of the finest I'd ever seen and his uncle's company brought in a lot of revenue. Though he obviously had money, there was no way he had that type of cash to invest.

"You have that in the bank."

T.J. shuffled his body as a smile broke across his face. "Not exactly, but I have it." He leaned closer, dropped his voice down a few octaves and said, "The feds aren't going to look at Noire, Inc. if I give you the cash. My money would just blend in with your clean money. I'll just be a silent partner."

The truth had finally come out. I didn't know T.J. well, but I should have figured his money was as dirty as the south. Only a young hustler would try to circumvent the law just to fulfill their street dreams. I didn't want to get involved, but I didn't want to say no. My ambition was stronger than my conscience.

"I'll think about it," I said.

"You do that." T.J. stood as the V.I.P. room door opened. "While you're thinking, relax. Because this *is* the time and the place."

T.J walked out of the room, leaving me to my own devices. As he departed, the lights were dimmed again and the sound of R. Kelly's voice escaped the speakers as he sung *Honey Love*. A spotlight went to a private stage in the middle of the room. Nasty had come out slowly gyrating her hips.

She wore a cowboy hat, white thongs, and a pair of black suede chaps. She captivated my total concentration as she balanced her body on the gleaming steel pole, spinning herself around it like it was second nature. And she finished her set by doing a split on the stage.

She was thick, but didn't have an ounce of fat on her. Her physique was solid. Though her breasts were small, her ample backside made up for it. Lust was in my eyes and it reeked from my skin.

There was nothing worse than a man in lust. There would be nothing that would get in the way of fulfilling my desire. She was my desire and I wanted to become one with her. I wanted to feel like a man again and conquer her.

She got on her knees and crawled in my direction. Her eyes were on me as she glided her tongue across her teeth. Her movements were smooth and precise and within moments, she had crawled her way to my lap. I tried helping her out, but she wanted control and pushed my hand to the side. Within moments, I was helpless to her powers.

CHAPTER FOURTEEN

Widow

I was in real love once in my life. Thinking back on that time, I could only remember it as the most beautiful experience in my existence. It was the purest of memories, providing my life with worth and purpose. Even the nightmares of my rape began to subside when I was in Thomas' arms. There was no place that I would rather be.

It was the one moment in my life when I let my guard down and allowed my heart to be stolen, but what had taken place in the aftermath caused me to wish that I'd listened to my mother when she gave me that advice. I didn't, thus I was doomed to be haunted by that memory for the rest of my life. I often wondered how I made it without him. After Thomas' death, I was in a daze and I numbed that pain by sexing strange men. Now, I couldn't get that memory out of my head…

"Baby, you surely are something fine to look at." Thomas smiled as he rubbed me down with lotion.

"I'm glad you think so."

"No. The world would think you're beautiful. I'm just lucky to have you by my side."

A gentle breeze blew in from off the waterfront through the windows, baptizing my body with goose bumps. Bohemian incense burned as Al Green played in the background.

I wore nothing while lying in his bed, spread eagle as he catered to me. The bedroom was in complete darkness; the only glimmer of light came from the incense, the moon, and the stars. Thomas leased the home only a week earlier in a secluded part of Brandon, Mississippi overlooking the waterfront, where my moans wouldn't disturb anyone, a place where we were sheltered from injury.

The atmosphere was enticing. It made me want to give myself to him on a silver platter without any inhibitions, but I didn't want to rush. I wanted to enjoy the moment, wanted to feel the brilliance of his movements. Thomas took his time when seducing me. He never came on too strong or aggressive. Foreplay was just as important as the act of sex and unlike most men, he spared nothing.

Thomas' hands were simply magical as he kneaded my body gently, performing the art of a Balinese massage. His touch was gentle yet strong.

I'd never met anyone quiet like him. He was a man that could be forceful and loving at the same time and balance both beautifully. A derogatory word never left his lips when it came to me and it wasn't an act. I saw it in his eyes. He loved me and I knew it.

This wasn't supposed to be like this. He was supposed to be another mark; another man that met the sharp end of my blade, but something fell over me. I thought I could control love. I thought that if I tried to hate every man I met, love's curse would never enslave me. But I was wrong, horribly wrong, and I didn't know what to do about it.

Thomas wasn't a great man. By all accounts, he was nothing more than a murderer and a drug dealer. Yet his occupation didn't matter to me, nor did the fact that he was known as a man that possessed an unapologetic temper. He treated me like a queen and someone he couldn't live without. That was what I needed to be to a man. I needed to be irreplaceable.

"You treat me so good."

"I treat you the way you make me feel," he complimented, bending down to nibble on my ear.

I looked at him and loved the symmetry of muscles that peeked from his shirt. Though he was sixty-five, his body was on point and as the old saying goes *"Black don't crack"*.

"Why don't you join me?"

He slowly removed each article of clothing as I watched longingly, from the money green long sleeve silk shirt down to the gray gabardine pants and black Gucci moccasins. He had set me ablaze by the time his boxer briefs hit the floor.

"First, I have a surprise for you," he said, running out of the master bedroom, down the spiral staircase. I sighed out of frustration, not because I wanted him sexually, but I felt safe when he was near me.

There was much more to our relationship than sex. We had a connection, the type of connection that transcended age or reason. Most onlookers couldn't comprehend our affinity for each other. To some, my love was based strictly on what he could do for me materially and to others, his love was based on what I could do for him sexually. But they were wrong. We were soulmates, soulmates that were lucky enough to meet before the next life.

Sometimes, I wanted to believe that it was too good to be true. In my mind, there had to be a flaw to his love, a defect hidden beyond the scope of my vision. But no matter how thoroughly I searched, I couldn't find a reason to believe that this feeling wasn't real.

My crew wanted me to kill him. They wanted him put to death. The deed was supposed to be completed a week earlier, but I couldn't. I couldn't kill a man that I had so much affection for. So I lied to Thomas. I told him that we needed to get a way. We needed to go somewhere and enjoy each other's bodies for nights on end. That was what I told him.

The lights came on, nearly blinding me. When I regained full sight, a smile emerged across Thomas' lips as he walked over the threshold. But he didn't budge and the smile only grew more prominent. Suddenly, I distinguished the small black velvet box in his hand.

I jumped up with my eyes beginning to water as I lost the breath inside of me. He walked closer, moving for the first time as he opened the box. The diamond shimmered and every fleck glistened with each of his measured movements.

I brought my hands to my mouth. I wanted to scream. That was the moment I had dreamed about as a little girl. My dreams were always so vivid that I remembered them as if they had really happened. Only, I had never seen the face of the man in my dreams, but at that instant, I knew it was Thomas.

He got on his knees, grazed my legs with his palm and he looked into my eyes with honesty. We talked about him giving up his lifestyle. He said that he'd consider it when he settled down. This was his gesture. This was how he wanted to live the rest of his life.

"Will you marry me, Garcelle?" His eyes were misty as he mouthed those words.

"Yes, baby. Yes." I jumped on him and wrapped my arms around his neck, nearly pushing him to the ground.

My feelings were unexplainable. I thought I had lost the opportunity for marriage. I thought I was worthless and used up. I felt no man would ever want to give himself to a woman like me, a woman that had her innocence stolen so violently. I was so overjoyed. I could barely stop crying.

"I'm happy, only if you're happy," he whispered in my ear as I trembled in his arms.

"We have to celebrate. We have to enjoy this moment." I instantly turned anxious, not knowing how to exactly react. My head was spinning. I could hardly stay still as I thought about the wedding plans.

He firmly grabbed hold of me. "Don't get all crazy on me. Just slow down and take it all in. I'm gonna need you to be the level headed one in this relationship. There's no telling how long we have before I go senile," he said with a smile on my face.

"As long as this doesn't go senile on me, I'll be fine," I said, pointing at his heart

"Is that all you care about?" he asked while rubbing my shoulders down with each of his hands.

"I love you. I'll be with you whether you can get it up or not."

"You better."

He went downstairs and I danced in the middle of the bedroom. My body felt as light as a feather. I felt like I could walk on water. I envisioned walking down the aisle in a white dress, as Thomas waited for me at the altar. The wedding march would play and I would be the focus of everyone's attention, and a smile would be on his face, because I was the woman he wanted to spend the rest of his life with.

Minutes went by and Thomas still hadn't come back upstairs. I thought I'd surprise him, run up on him when he didn't expect it, and take him right in the kitchen on top of the dining room table. I blew out the incense, closed the windows, and walked down the back staircase by the kitchen. It was dark when I got downstairs and Thomas was nowhere to be found.

"Thomas, stop playing around. I'm horny as hell," I said, my voice echoing throughout the entire downstairs.

I heard rustling, felt a breeze, and noticed that the front door was open. I walked across the hardwood floor, my feet sticking to the wood with each step. When I made it to the front door I looked outside, but there was still no one to be found. He was naked, so I knew he wasn't outside. He just wanted to play games.

"Thomas, you better stop playing with me. Don't mess this night up after you made it so special."

I was beginning to get mad. I could feel my skin go flush and my muscles tense. That was when I smelled his blood. I looked down at my feet and realized. I was standing in a puddle of his blood, a puddle that led into the great room.

I'd seen and smelled blood many times before and it had never bothered me, but this time nausea took control of me. I vomited in the middle of the floor. The great room door was locked. My legs could barely move and I didn't want to look inside, because I knew what I'd see. I didn't want to see him like that.

I opened the door, and I was hit with another strong whiff of the blood that assaulted my nostrils. His body lay on the floor, his headless body. A message was written in his blood on the off white walls. It read, "*N.B.D. was here.*"

I knew then that my time was limited. Someone was still in the house, because the blood hadn't dried and my crew always searched room to room thoroughly. Money always came first. They were in the garage and I had managed to avoid their ears and eyes. Quietly, I searched Thomas' pants as I tried to stifle my tears.

In my nakedness, I ran for the door while searching the key ring for the correct key. Turning back to say goodbye to my love, I, instead, locked stares with the masked killer. The eyes belonged to a woman. I had already been replaced. She didn't challenge me. In fact, she didn't even reach for the bulge on the side of her hips. She'd gotten what she came for. I would be collateral damage. *N.B.D.* didn't like unnecessary deaths. Unwarranted deaths only made it harder to disappear. They only killed who they came for, but I knew they'd come for me next.

I ran across the lawn bare foot and naked. I opened the car door, locked stares with the female again as she stood on the front steps glaring at me. I started the car. The Cadillac revved up as I hit the gas, leaving tire marks on the blacktop.

Tears flowed down my face, smearing my mascara and leaving a trail of black down my cheeks. I wanted to drive off the highest bridge. I didn't want to live. I couldn't live without Thomas. The man of my dreams no longer had a breath in his body and neither did I. My future husband was dead, making me a widow. I drove in the darkness until I couldn't drive anymore…Knowing I'd be back one day for revenge.

CHAPTER FIFTEEN

Julian

    I departed from Atlanta without reaching a deal with T.J., though he showed me a great time, there was no way I was going to bring his element into my establishment. I'd just have to find a way to make my next project come to fruition without his money. I had integrity and there was no way I was going to go against my gut feeling. And that was why I wasn't going to fall victim to Carl's blackmail tactics. He wouldn't get a dime from me. He'd have to find Simone's body to prove that I killed her. He only had pictures that could have been photo shopped.

    When I got back to the office the day after my trip to Atlanta, Andrea was waiting for me. I didn't know what to say to her. It seemed like every time we got close she pulled further away. That bothered me. I didn't know if I could work with that. What would I do if I really fell in love? I couldn't take any more rejection.

On the plane ride back, I felt the best course of action would be if we stopped talking. I had already rehearsed my speech, but when I saw her standing there dressed in a black business suit and high heels that brought out her well toned calves, I lost all composure.

"Sorry," she said getting up from one of the seats in the waiting room.

"Is that the way you're always going to greet me?"

"Can we have some privacy?" she asked noticing the way my secretary perked up as we spoke.

"Sheila, hold my calls," I ordered my secretary, as I opened the door to my office.

I took a look at Andrea as she sashayed into the room. She just didn't know the affect she had on me.

"Take a seat," I offered as I extended my hand towards the set of chairs across from my desk.

Tension lived in the room as we remained in silence with eyes challenging the other to speak first. I decided to remain standing, giving the impression that I didn't want our conversation to last too long. If the conversation took a wrong turn, it wouldn't take much to escort her out.

I hoped it wouldn't come to that. If there was a way she could explain her hot and cold behavior, I wanted to hear it. That was something I always regretted about the way I gave up on my marriage. I never gave Miko a chance to explain herself. A woman with frustration built up will only look for other ways to release it.

"What do you want to talk about?" I wanted to hear her out, but at the same time, I really wanted to know whether or not she had someone else in her life, someone she had neglected to tell me about.

She crossed her legs, unknowingly showing off her magnificent chocolate thighs. "I quit my job," she revealed, searching my face for compassion.

"What happened? I thought you loved your job."

Tears started to flow from her eyes. I wanted to rush to her side and put my arm over her shoulder, but I wasn't sure if she wanted that type of affection. I learned earlier that her emotions were pretty unstable.

"I'm burnt out. I'm just not happy." She shook her head searching for answers.

Knowing that she had come to me looking for a shoulder to cry on made me feel important. I knew she hadn't made any friends since leaving Atlanta or had any parents. The fact that she chose me to expose her vulnerability really meant something to me.

"Let's get out of here," I ordered, knowing exactly how to cheer her up. That was the main perk to being my own boss. I made my own hours.

"And go where?" she asked, wiping at the tears in the corner of her eyes.

"To someone I want you to meet," I said, reaching out for her hand.

Aasia screamed as soon as we entered the house and Natalie wasn't far behind. They were in the midst of playing hide and go seek and Natalie had obviously been it. I was happy to see that they were having fun and that was what I wanted for my daughter. She deserved to have a happy childhood, unlike the one I had to endure.

Aasia had finally decided that being a princess had worn itself out and was now dressed like I imagined any little girl should, wearing a plaid one piece swimsuit with flip flops.

Joining in the fun, I bent down and lifted her off the ground.

"Aasia, I want you to meet my friend," I said as Natalie tagged her on the arm to her dismay.

I'd never brought a woman home to meet Aasia, because I never met one that I thought I could actually be with. Andrea was slowly becoming that one. Though I still barely knew her, our connection was real. If she worked through her trust issues, I could see us together. I could envision her as my next wife.

Admitting that I was falling hard was difficult, but what was even more difficult was living life alone. I wanted a second chance, a second time to fall in love with a special lady and treat her the way she deserved to be treated. That would relieve the guilt that I felt in my heart for ignoring Miko for so long.

Andrea stood in the foyer with a radiant smile on her face as we approached. "This is my princess," I said, introducing my two women.

"You are adorable." Andrea cooed reaching out for Aasia's hand, but Aasia pulled away. Instead, she buried her head in my chest. "Say hi to Ms. Youngblood," I requested softly;

Aasia buried her face in my chest and shook her head across my collarbone, refusing to look at Andrea. I felt bad. I didn't understand why Aasia was acting anti-social, especially since she had been doing so well.

Natalie stepped in. "Hello, I'm Natalie. Do you work together?" she asked Andrea in an icy tone.

"No, we are friends," Andrea explained.

There was an uncomfortable vibe between the two. It was almost like they were sizing each other up. I didn't know either of them really well, but I got the feeling that their first impressions of each other weren't great. They'd already decided that they didn't care for each other without knowing one another.

Aasia was troubled; usually, she was able to tell someone what she thought of them while looking that person in the eye, but she couldn't look at Andrea and I wanted to know why.

"You two get to know each other. I'm gonna talk to my daughter." I left them standing in the foyer as I carried Aasia into her bedroom.

I could feel dampness cover my dress shirt as I carried her in the room. That hurt my heart; nothing bothered me more than to see my princess cry. It did something to me when I thought of her being harmed or feeling pain. Like a loving father, I always wanted to protect her. But as she grew, I realized there were things I could never protect her from.

Entering her room, I lifted her in the air and stared at her compassionately as she wiped at her eyelids with her delicate little hands.

"You alright?" I asked, placing a kiss on her face as I stepped over toys that were scattered about. She didn't say anything, just remained silent.

Setting her down on her poster bed and parting the white curtains that hung down, I asked her again, "You alright, sweetness?"

I sat next to her wondering what could be on the mind of a four-year-old that was so troubling. If she wanted to know real pain, wait till she grew up.

"Are you gonna talk to Daddy?" I asked while wiping the tears that she had missed.

She sniffled, cleared her throat, and said, "I don't like her."

"Beautiful, she's a nice lady. Daddy likes her." I held her chin up as I looked down into her face. Aasia pulled away and let another tidal wave of tears flow down her cheeks.

I consoled her, but didn't know what to say. I heard horror stories that girls were overprotective of their fathers, but this was different.

"I hate her," Aasia cried.

"Don't say that. You never say that about anybody," I chastised. "Do you want Daddy to be happy?"

It was unusual to ask a child's opinion on personal matters, but I wanted her to understand that I had feelings, as well. "Why can't you be happy with Mommy?" she whined.

At that moment, I understood exactly what her problem was about, but I couldn't phrase the reality of her mother's death in a way she could understand. I dodged questions about Miko like Muhammad Ali dodged left hooks.

"Mommy can't be with daddy now, but one day I'll be with Mommy again."

"Like that lady?" She perked up.

Small children aren't given the credit they deserve; some are very smart and perceptive.

There was a picture of Miko on her nightstand. I reached out my hand and grabbed the gold plated frame and looked at my late wife. I remembered her dark, flawless complexion and her voracious appetite. I wondered if I'd ever meet her equal.

"Who's this?" I asked. Aasia pulled the frame from my grip and stared at her mother. I felt it was about time to really talk to her about her mother and what type of person she was.

"That's Mommy."

"Where is Mommy?" She pointed to her heart.

"Who does Mommy love, very, very much?" I asked again.

"Me." Aasia pointed at her chest as her face began to lighten up.

"And who does Daddy love, very, very much?"

"Me." She pointed at herself again grinning from ear to ear.

"Good." I took the photo and placed it in-between us. "And Daddy loves Mommy too. Can you keep a secret? " I whispered.

"Yep."

"Daddy won't love anybody else like Mommy."

That made her day. She outstretched her arms and I hugged her, knowing that one day the both of us would learn to live without Miko.

I spent the rest of the morning with Andrea walking along the Biscayne Shore. It was a beautiful day. The sun illuminated us with its rays as we held hands while enjoying the beautiful waterfront view. A live band played Latin music at daybreak, making the setting of the sun festive climax. Watching the sun turn the sky into an eclectic hue of oranges, pinks and purples turned our evening into a night to remember.

I enjoyed her company and I got to know a lot more about her. I didn't realize that she'd taken care of her ailing mother until her death. That explained why she feared giving her heart away, because everyone she had ever cared about had gone asleep in death.

I didn't feel the same way when it came to death. I had learned to accept the possibility of it. Andrea had fond memories of her mother. On the other hand, I had nothing but terrible memories of my father. He'd literally killed the two women I needed most, my mother and Miko. Though he didn't kill my mother with his hands, he killed her with his unyielding stubbornness, but they all were better off, because they were underground where death, pain, and the recession couldn't touch them.

Her interest in my job was astounding. Most women could care less what I did for a living as long as I made a great deal of money, but she actually wondered what it took to build a hotel from concept to completion. It felt good to talk about my passion for a change. With the business end of the business becoming so difficult, I almost forgot how much I loved architecture.

Andrea made the right move by quitting her job. Sometimes, acclaim came with a cost. I remembered my days at The Denzler Group and

Associates. I was unfulfilled. My skills were taken for granted and I felt worthless. Those feelings, which I held inside, pushed me into a world that I was unfamiliar with, one that still gave me nightmares. I loved success, but sometimes I craved the days when my life was simple.

Our night ended with a simple kiss that lingered until we had to come up for air. I hated to see the night end without exploring the undiscovered parts of her anatomy, but I didn't want to rush the inevitable. It would be only a matter of time before she surrendered her body to me.

My eyes were at half-mast when I entered my home. I was ready for bed and I couldn't wait until I was able to dream about some of the things that I wanted to do to Andrea. Natalie was standing in front of the television doing a Tae Bo workout routine when I walked into the family room. She was dressed in only a North Carolina University baby blue sports bra and a pair of oversized basketball shorts. I could feel my face go flush as she swung at a make-believe assailant.

When she realized I was watching, she turned down the television and wiped her face with a towel. "How long have you been here?"

she wondered as she held the towel over her exposed stomach.

"Long enough to know that I don't want to get into a fight with you…"

"Don't be so modest. You're in pretty good shape."

"Only pretty good shape?" I flirted, noticing beads of sweat traveling down her bra.

"Great shape…" She smiled. "Now, have I inflated your head enough?"

There were other parts of my body that she was inflating besides my head and as I held my briefcase over my groin area, I wondered if she noticed. I put my briefcase down and took my shoes off.

She grabbed a water bottle and plopped down on the couch. "Can I ask you a question, Julian?"

"Sure," I answered nervously, wondering if she had noticed the bulge. I didn't need sexual harassment charges on top of murder charges that Carl wanted to pin on me.

"I'm not trying to overstep my boundaries, but there's something not right about your friend."

"What do you mean?"

"She just doesn't seem to be who she says she is," Natalie admonished.

I sat down wanting to hear how she stumbled upon such an extreme assumption.

"Did she say anything when the two of you were alone to make you think that?"

Natalie leaned forward, cracking her knuckles with crow's feet embedded on the sides of her eyelids. "No, but there was something about her; I could tell by looking in her eyes that she was a liar or living a lie."

I didn't want to totally discount what Natalie was saying, because Andrea had given me that vibe, as well, but at the same time, people judged me wrong, as well. You could never know who a person truly is even if you live with them. Miko had taught me that.

"I appreciate your concern, but I'm only getting to know her. It's nothing serious."

"It's serious enough for you bring her home to meet your daughter."

I swallowed hard; she had now overstepped that boundary that she treaded earlier. Probably sensing my irritation, she stood and turned off the television. With her back to me, I could make out the outline of her behind through the fabric of the shorts she wore. They were baggy but still accentuated her luscious curves.

She walked towards me, stopping in front of me only inches from my face. The scent of her sweaty body released pheromones that enticed my erotic senses.

I didn't know why, but my hands went to the bottom of her knees and traveled up to her thigh. She removed the glasses from her face, removed the ribbon that held her bun in place and let her hair fall to her shoulders and down her back. Her tresses were long, a lot longer than I'd visualized and her face was beautiful, a lot more gorgeous than I'd envisioned. She grabbed my hand, led me to the storage closet in the kitchen where she removed her bra.

" Is this cool?" she asked, before letting her tongue go in and out my ear canal.

"It's...cool." That was all I could mutter as she began to discard my belt from around my waist.

I wanted control, so I spun her around, kissing along her spine. Her skin was as soft as a child's. That was until...I noticed the burns, the burns on her back, the burns that could have only been put there by someone else.

CHAPTER SIXTEEN

Widow

Julian knew how to make a woman feel special; unfortunately, he would end up just like the rest. A conscience didn't have a damn thing to do with my cash flow. It was just too bad, because he did the damn thang. I hadn't gotten treated like that since, well, since Thomas. Julian wasn't as smooth as Thomas was, but I got the impression that if Julian didn't have any money, he wouldn't know how to get a woman to sleep with him. He was a square, too boring for me, but he knew how to get me upset just like any other man.

He had the nerve to bring Ms. Prissy into the house. I just didn't like home girl. There was something suspicious about Andrea. I could tell that she was putting on an act; only, she didn't do it too well. I put on an act just about every time I woke in the morning, so I knew how it looked when someone else was doing the same. She sure enough was stealing my style, black wasn't her color.

Maybe she had a man on the side or wanted to take him for his money, but that was his problem; if he was going to let his penis lead him in the wrong direction, then he deserved what was going to transpire. At the end of the day, I didn't care whether or not she played Julian. It wasn't like he was going to live long enough to experience the pain of rejection.

The only problem this assignment had given me was the feelings I was gaining for Aasia. A child wasn't my thing, but she grew on me. I loved spending time with her. When we went on walks together, most people mistook me for her mother. I didn't realize how much I liked that feeling, the feeling of living for someone other than myself.

Taking her father from her would be my only regret, but she stood to inherit millions. I was sure she'd find someway to kill time as she grew up. At least, she wouldn't grow up the way I did.

When I awakened, Julian was beside me. We were in his office on the floor wrapped in a quilt. The lingering smell of sex scented my flesh as I stirred. I barely remembered how we ended up on the cold marble floors, but I attributed that to the empty bottle of vodka lying beside me.

A tiny slit of light tried to squeeze into the room through the closed blinds. As my eyes adjusted to the darkness, I noticed the time on the antique wall clock that sat above his desk. It was nearly noon and we both had forgotten about

Aasia and that terrified me. I kicked at the quilt with my legs, awaking Julian in the process.

"What's…going on?" Julian mouthed, waking from a liquor-induced slumber.

"Look at the time. That's what's going on," I said, searching his office for any signs of my clothing.

With squinty eyes, he searched for the clock. A look of terror spread across his face as he discovered the time and he too joined me in a search for our clothing. That's when we heard something we dreaded, the sound of a tiny fist knocking on the office door.

"Daddy, Daddy, its me, Aasia." She sounded scared. The same angst in her voice as I carried the day my father left my mother and I.

I remembered that day, remembered it like it was yesterday. It was the first time a man had left me. He didn't only leave my mother but me, as well. That always tore at my heart, made me wonder if I was worth staying for. I always heard of men staying in bad marriages for the sake of their children. My father hadn't done that for me. Julian looked at me and I returned his glare. He pointed at the door, wanting me to say something, but I didn't know what to say. How could I explain walking out with her father, the both of us naked? Or would I have to explain it at all?

"Aasia?" I said in the syrupy tone that she enjoyed.

"Natalie, Natalie, I'm hungry," she sobbed. Her vulnerability made my stomach do flips, made me territorial. I hated to see her in pain.

"Go upstairs and turn on cartoons and I'll be right there." I comforted her.

"Where is Daddy? He didn't say goodbye this morning."

I looked at Julian; he stuck out his arms, just as clueless as I was at that moment.

"He's doing something. He's going to be right back. Okay, sweetie."

"Can I look at Scooby Doo?"

"If you want." I looked at Julian again for some help, but he was of no assistance. "Go upstairs and I'll get you something to eat.

I listened to her tiny feet walk across the floor until the sound disappeared.

        I felt a little better hearing her voice. I could only imagine the abandonment she felt as she walked from room to room in search of Julian and I.

"Where are my clothes?" I asked Julian, ripping the quilt from his clutches. "This is mine. You better find something to put on.

"I remember just as much as you do," he said looking around as I watched his movements, taking in the flexibility of his limber body.

"Good luck," I said, smacking his behind just as hard as he smacked mine the night before.

When I reached the top of the steps, Aasia was glued to the television sitting Indian style dressed in a pink, cotton gown, clutching the zebra that I bought for her. I stood at the top of the stairs and watched her. She was so innocent, so undefiled and filled with love.

Possibly hearing my footsteps, she turned from her cartoon and smiled at me with love in her eyes. That gave me a chill.

"Why you dressed like that?" She laughed at the quilt wrapped around my body.

"I 'm cold." I lied.

"You look funny."

"You are so mean," I said as I acted like I was crying wiping at my eyes.

She ran to me and wrapped me in a tiny hug as I massaged the top of her head. I reminisced on the days when I was her age when my mother was young and happy, before my father's departure and the diabetes robbed her of her vitality. Those were the days I held on to when I remembered my mother. I didn't like remembering her when she was sick, because it reminded me of my own mortality.

"What do you want to eat?" I asked kneeling down and fixing her hair.

"I want cereal. The one with the marshmallows."
She jumped up and down.

"What did I tell you about calling things by their proper name?" I said, taking her chin in my hands.

"I want Lucky Charms."

"That's good."

I opened the storage closet and it looked like it had been ransacked. Boxes and cans were everywhere. Cereal was on the floor and my clothes were strewn about. Just at that moment, Julian had finally made an appearance making his way to the top of the steps dressed in a dingy white sweat suit that looked like he'd found it somewhere behind the boiler.

"What's my princess doing?" he said, lifting Aasia and spinning her around in his arms.

"Natalie's gonna make me cereal." Aasia said, pecking her father on the cheek

"Is that right?" Julian laughed.

"No, I'm gonna cook for you both," he offered.

I closed the closet door and rolled my eyes in disbelief. "Now I got to see this. I didn't know you had cooking skills."

"You know, I got skills," he flirted. "You two get in the kitchen and take a seat," he said, carrying Aasia to the table as I followed behind.

He set Aasia in her seat and opened the refrigerator door. Sticking his head inside, he rummaged for ingredients to make his so-called breakfast or what according to the time would be known as brunch.

Initially, I heard glass breaking and it wasn't because Julian dropped anything to the floor. It was because the sound was too far off, but it started to get closer. That's when I heard a popping sound, the sound of a semi-automatic weapon. My first move wasn't to protect my own welfare. Instead, I jumped for Aasia, grabbed her, and covered her with my body as we fell to the floor.

Bullets riddled the kitchen just as Julian jumped to the floor, as well, forgetting to close the refrigerator door behind him. As Aasia cried out loud, I heard the sound of bullets whizzing just over us. The sound of the high powered weapon's force as its slugs pierced the walls and punctured the food in the refrigerator had drowned out her wails.

Then it stopped. The shooting had ended and there was utter silence. Aasia was silent as well. I shook her, but she didn't move, and she no longer cried.

CHAPTER SEVENTEEN

Julian

While Aasia lay limply on the floor, my heart was in my chest, but she was fine. There was no damage done to her, at least not physically. I had she and Natalie sent to Frederick's house. They would be safe there. The police came and searched the premises. I told them that I didn't know anything and that I didn't have any enemies that I knew of. I could tell they didn't believe me, but they had nothing else to go on.

Carl gave me twenty-four hours and I didn't heed the warning. I let my ego and stubbornness over take conventional wisdom. Carl was just plain crazy. Though I feared that Carl wouldn't stop at anything to get to his money, I never thought he'd put my daughter's welfare at risk, but I forgot that the love of money rarely came with pity.

Afterward, I called Frederick to set up a meeting with T.J. I needed cash badly and hopefully, he could supply the cash that I needed to get out of this situation. T.J. had access to the type of money that would be undetected by the federal government. I didn't need them getting involved. I didn't know how much Carl had on me or how far it went. I wanted to pay him and hoped that would be enough.

I knew Carl's location. He had a small accounting firm that he started to make extra money on the side. It was in Little Havana, the rough side of town. I could easily take him the money and end all the madness.

It felt like my life was moving in slow motion as I sat in my office watching the cars sixteen stories below. This feeling was surreal. Wasn't riches supposed to protect you from danger and put me in a place where the riff raff of the world couldn't touch me? Instead, it seemed like since I started on my road to riches that it brought nothing but pain and hurt in its aftermath.

I barely noticed Frederick walk into my office, only felt nervousness consume me as the door slammed.

"You alright?" he asked consolingly.

"I'm straight," I said in an undertone, rubbing the five o' clock shadow that covered my face.

"T.J. will be here soon," Frederick said walking towards me with compassion in his eyes. "I don't know how you can be so composed about this. I think we should just get rid of the problem."

I knew he meant well, but I also knew that the carnage would never cease. I didn't want to go that route once again. I didn't want to give someone the opportunity to hold another death over me. This had to stop and it had to stop with Carl.

"But you aren't me. So let it be," I commanded. I didn't need anyone telling me what to do or not to do with the situation. I could live with my own decisions not anyone else's.

My composure belied the fact that I was fuming. My blood simmered beneath the surface. I once again felt less than a man, because I had to turn the other cheek, once again. I had allowed another person to devastate my life and walk away without any retribution. But there was no other way and the only other way was not an option.

Frederick paced back and forth across my office. There was a tense expression on his face, as he bit on his nails. He was just as nervous as I was. I didn't need that at the moment. Nervousness was like a cancer. It spread quickly and I needed all the strength I could muster.

There was a knock at the door and T.J. entered with a stern look on his face, providing the type of strength I needed. I could tell that he detested men that harmed children. He'd possibly come from an upbringing where he was exposed to violence, an upbringing that molded his violent ways.

He entered with a briefcase containing the money that I needed to get rid of the problem. I stood and we embraced like men do, with one arm as we shook hands with the other. That gesture told me all that I needed to know about T.J. He was a man of loyalty. He had made my pain his pain.

He placed the briefcase across my desk and popped the locks, revealing stacks of hundred dollar bills and a contract. The contract was our agreement that he'd have an interest in Atlanta Noiree. I wanted to add an extra "E" to each of my new buildings to symbolize the word *eternity,* because they would be around long after I had been laid to rest.

I didn't care to read over the contract. I was in such a frenzied state that I just signed my name on the dotted line. The only particulars that I cared about were whether or not I contained controlling interest, which I did.

There was definitely something amiss about Frederick. He was still acting too nervous and was beginning to concern me, so I asked him to allow T.J. and I to speak privately. I didn't know if I wanted him around for what I wanted to say.

I sat at my desk and T.J. sat across from me.

"I want this to end," I stated in my most serious tone. "I don't want this coming back."

"What are you saying?" T.J. asked.

My anger was beginning to get the best of me. Though I didn't want any blood shed, I knew if I continued to allow people to victimize me that I would always play the victim. It would be open season for any low life thug that wanted to get quick cash.

I did research on T.J. I found out that his father was a long time heroin dealer that made his fortune in the late seventies. He also ran a deadly gang of hit men. They controlled the drug trade and whoever stood in their way was quickly put to rest. His name was Thomas Willingham and T.J. was Thomas Willingham Jr. He was in charge of his father's gang now and was the leading distributor of narcotics in the south. I knew he could get rid of my problem for all eternity.

"I mean I want him taken care of," I said. A chill spread over me. It wasn't what I wanted to do. It was what I had to do.

A smile broke across T.J.'s face, the likes of which I had never seen. He had probably wanted to get rid of Carl to begin with. T.J. wasn't the sort of man that paid for anything to go away. Death was the only sure thing. As my father always said, a dead man tells no tales.

"No doubt, bruh, no doubt," he said leaning back in his chair as if my words were music to his ears. He didn't even need any more information; he said it was already taken care of.

Andrea was the only person that I felt I could talk to. I trusted her. She had confided in me and I felt I could do the same. We were behind Miami Noire in the same spot where we had nearly made love only a week prior. This time we weren't thinking about quenching our carnal thirst, nor did we care about the beautiful ambiance that surrounded us.

"I think I'm changing for the worst," I confided. As each day passed, I felt a change in my heart. It was like my heart was becoming numb to all of the dysfunction that surrounded me. For the first time, I had no feelings about Miko's death. It wasn't that I didn't think of her anymore, I just didn't feel the pain that had caused me to languish over the years.

"You're going through a lot. That's just the way you're feeling now." She reasoned, looking into my eyes for confirmation that she was right.

"No, I don't care the way I used to," I pointed at Miami Noire stretched out in its magnificence. "That used to mean something to me. I mean the love of creating something beautiful. Now, I only care about protecting what I have acquired."

I had a love of architecture as a child that consumed all my thoughts. I lived in a New York City project development and I used my imagination to take me to other surroundings. I would dream about creating a beautiful place for my father and I to live, so that we could escape the poverty that surrounded us. I could taste success as a child, but after attaining it, the love of my vision was starting to die and be replaced by the desire to never live in poverty again.

"You feel like that, because you don't know how to process your feelings. You keep things hidden inside."

"You're my psychiatrist now?"

"Yes and No. I've gone to a therapist, in the last week, just to get past these feelings I have about cheating on Bryant, even though he isn't alive. And..." She paused.

"And..." I said wanting her to finish her statement.

"She said that the reason I can't rid myself of those feelings is because I haven't faced up to them. I used work to cover over my guilt. You are doing the same. You're using work to cover over your guilt."

Maybe she was right. I felt a burden that wanted to come out. I needed to talk, so I did, telling her every sordid detail of my life over the last five years.

CHAPTER EIGHTEEN

Widow

"Meet me at 12 Northwest Thirty-sixth Street. Come in through the front. I'll be in the apartment all the way in the back." My client spoke with an edge to his voice. "Bring the girl with you," He spat.

"She'll just slow me down," I reasoned.

"Bring her. We need her here. She's an integral part of the plan."

"What about Julian? This is supposed to be about him."

"If you bring the girl, he won't be far behind," he said before hanging up abruptly.

I wondered why they needed Aasia there. I understood that she could be used as bait to lure Julian, but it could get messy. She had already been through enough. There was no way I was going to put her in harm's way. I would bring her, but I would make sure she would be some place safe.

I looked around Frederick's condominium. I was at home in the cold surroundings. It was the typical bachelor pad, devoid of color and warmth. The walls were white washed and the furniture was leather, black leather. Every vase painting and light fixture was in pristine condition, there wasn't even a fingerprint on the floor to the ceiling glass that overlooked Biscayne Bay.

I walked into the kitchen where teak wood and stainless steel came together. Aasia was sitting at the table staring at the cereal I had given her. She was motionless; it was almost like she'd been hypnotized. She hadn't said a thing since the shooting. She bore the look I possessed the night I'd been raped.

I wasn't sure how we were going to get out of Frederick's apartment. Julian had hired an armed security guard to watch over us after the shooting had taken place, but I had an idea. I knew of one place where he couldn't follow us. Only, I had to get downstairs to make my plan work.

I looked ordinary, dressed in a pair of oversized sweats I had hijacked from Frederick's closet. My hair was down and I had decided to apply my makeup lightly, but I still knew I could get the job done for what I had in mind.

"Do you want to go down to the pool?" I asked Aasia as she watched the cornflakes turn to mush.
She didn't say anything; she just clutched her stuffed zebra. She hadn't let go of it since the shooting. I lifted her in the air, grabbed my purse, and kissed her on the cheeks. As I exited his

condo, I was stopped by one of Julian's hired men. He was tall, chocolate and bald. I could tell that a little persuasion would be in order.

He was dressed like an extra in Men in Black. He wore a black suit, white shirt, black tie, and a pair of aviator sunglasses.

"Hello handsome. What's your name?" I smiled, stroking his ego as I pressed the button calling for the elevator.

"I'm Marvin and I'm under strict orders to make sure no one comes and goes," he said reaching for the bulge in his jacket as the elevator doors opened.

I placed my hand on his bulging biceps, rubbed my hand across the length of his arms, and said, "She wants to dip her feet in the pool. She's been so traumatized since the shooting I wanted to do something to take her mind off it," I said, appealing to his sensitive side, but he obviously had none since he didn't even flinch.

He looked at me suspiciously and then glanced down at Aasia as I placed her to the floor. "I'm sorry, ms, but I can't allow that," he said as though there was no way he was going to let us go. Only, he didn't know that I was leaving even if it had to be over his dead body.

I sighed, this was going to be harder than I expected. I needed to think quickly. I looked down at his shoes. I noticed that they were scuffed and worn. You could tell a lot about a man by the condition of their shoes. He was definitely hard up for cash.

I reached into my purse, grazed the tip of my blade as the possibility of using it crossed my mind and took out two crisp one hundred dollar bills. There was no need for further convincing as I watched in amazement when he fell for the bait.

He followed us to the pool. There was no way he was going to leave us alone and I counted on that.

"She has to use the ladies room," I said glancing up.

"Okay, but leave your purse," he demanded.

I didn't want to, but there was no other way. I could see that he wasn't going to relent. I rummaged through my bag, stuffed my knife and the smart key to Frederick's Mercedes as far as I could inside a maxi pad.

"Okay, but I need a few of my feminine products," I said as he scrunched his nose in horror as I extracted the maxi pad from my purse.

The purse was useless to me otherwise. It was part of my disguise. Besides, I didn't have any identification, at least not at the moment.

I picked Aasia up, once again, as he followed us to the bathroom entrance. Unfortunately for him, the bathroom had two exits. I entered one end and walked out the other.

He was none the wiser as I walked out the front of the building into broad daylight.

12 Northwest Thirty-sixth Street was the address of a run down apartment building in Little Havana on a block full of run down buildings on the outskirts of the Miami River. It was a ghost town. The building had obviously seen better days. It was a two-story structure with busted windows, some of which were boarded up with plywood, and the outside was littered with shattered glass bottles, brown paper bags, and food containers. The front door was slightly ajar, revealing a dark entrance where anything could happen. It was the sort of place one entered but never left alive.

I drove around the block a few times looking for any other signs of life. Yet, there were none to be found. I couldn't even call my client, because I left my phone in the purse. I always used prepaid cell phones to make contact with my clients and discarded them after my assignments completion. There was no way it could be traced back to me.

I looked at Aasia through the rear view mirror. I made sure she was strapped in her seat before I parked the Mercedes in an abandoned lot in the back of the building. I rolled the windows down slightly and got out the vehicle. She'd be safe at least until I found out exactly what was going on.

I surveyed my surroundings carefully as I walked to the building, stepping over used diapers, urine and discarded syringes. When I entered, the pungent odor of stale urine overtook me. I covered my nose as I navigated my way through the dimly lit first floor. It was a long jagged hallway that contained many blind spots.

That's why I barely noticed her as she walked towards me. I only heard the sound of her heels tapping against the linoleum floors. We stared at each other for a moment. I remembered those eyes. I couldn't place them at the moment, but they were glued to my memory. We had met before, somewhere at one point in my life. Her slanted eyes searched my face revealing that she too felt the same way. She seemed at ease in the filthy surroundings, chewing gum as she ran her fingers through her blond hair, dressed in head to toe Dior and carrying a Louis Vuitton bag .On her left breast was a tattoo and it read *Nasty*.

She looked at me one last time before walking out into the deserted street from which I came. I refocused my attention on the situation at hand. And after a few more steps, I reached the last door in the back of the building like I had been instructed. The apartment door was wide open. I knocked lightly, but there was no response. I walked further into the apartment as I heard voices coming from the background. My client was sitting in front of the television. I could tell by his trademark red fedora. He was sitting in a recliner with his back to me watching the news.

"What did you want to talk to me about?" I asked, looking around the apartment, wondering how a man paying me millions could live in such squalor. I hoped it was a place he had on the seedier part of town where he could do illegal transactions without suspicion.

I waited a minute, but he hadn't answered or budged.

"You hear me," I repeated. He didn't move.

Hating to be ignored, I stood in front of the television, turning it off as I crossed my arms around my chest. That's when I realized why he wasn't talking. He was dead, smiling with his neck. There was a deep gash across his throat. Unlike most death, it didn't shake me and the sight of blood didn't bother me, but there was an unshakable feeling of danger that coursed through my veins. I needed to get out of there.

In haste, I started to walk out of the front door, leaving behind the body of a man that was going to pay me a million. Now, it was feeling more like a set up. That was when I felt the steel against my temple, the cold steel.

CHAPTER NINETEEN

Julian

"Where is she?" I yelled with my hand wrapped around the collar of Marvin's suit. "They...they...went to the bathroom...then..." He tried to explain as I held him against the wall in Frederick's condo.

After T.J. called and told me he had personally taken care of my problem, I felt like the whole world had been lifted off my shoulder. That was until Marvin called and told me that Natalie had taken Aasia. I hoped that they would come back. I hoped they had gotten lost, but as the hours passed, so did my hopes. I couldn't even call the police. If they were able to link Carl to the shooting, they would probably be able to connect me to his death.

"You screwed up. You screwed up," I spewed. If something happened to Aasia I would hold him personally responsible.

There was no way to describe what I was feeling at that moment. My daughter was somewhere out there and I couldn't do anything about it. She could be hurt, cold, or hungry and I couldn't do a damn thing to protect her.

I released his collar, fell down to the floor, broke down, and cried. I hated myself for all the times I had taken my daughter for granted. I hated myself for not realizing that the past can come back to haunt me, no matter how far away I moved away from it.

I tried to breathe, but it felt like my airway was restricted. I gasped for air, tugging at my shirt as I tried to compose myself. I took a deep breath, calmed my nerves. I couldn't let the situation get the best of me. I had to be strong for Aasia.

My cellular phone rang. It was Andrea.

"Julian, I need to talk to you," she sounded rushed.

"Now is not the best time," I said as I rubbed my forehead.

I wanted to tell her what I was going through, but I didn't need her to overreact. Like any woman, her maternal instincts would probably take over and before I knew it Frederick's condo would be flooded with police. Besides, Frederick was roaming the streets for me, looking for any signs of Natalie and my daughter.

"What I have to say is very important. There is no better time," she said with anxiety in her tone.

I sighed, held the phone to my ear as tears blurred my vision. "Trust me, whatever you have to say to me can wait."

I had another incoming call. It was from Frederick's phone. "Hold on a moment," I said, clicking over.

"What's going on? Have you seen them?" I asked anxiously.

"I have them," he responded with trepidation in his voice.

"Is Aasia alright?" I asked, wanting to know if she was still in one piece.

"She's fine. I just need you to come down," he said with coldness in his voice.

"Where are you?" I asked, listening intently for any sounds in the background, wondering if he too was in some kind of trouble.

"I'm at Miami Noire, up by the roof top pool."

"Why are you up there? It's not even filled with water," I reasoned out of concern, but he never answered me as his line went dead.

There was no time to spare. I rushed to my car, silencing my phone as Andrea continued to call.

There was a storm brewing and the sound of the waves crashing against the rocks down below terrified me. The wind was fierce, blowing mightily against the cabanas that surrounded the pool, nearly turning them over as the curtains tossed in the wind. The roof was dark leaving me vulnerable to my surroundings. And the air was frigid, numbing my face as I searched for any sign of Frederick.

The pool area was still under construction. It was seventy five percent done, but it wasn't safe for a child.

When I felt the sensation of cold steel pressed against the back of my neck I realized someone had found me. I didn't turn around. I couldn't see the face of my captor, because any sudden movements would have most likely meant my death. The gun's barrel was pressed firmly against my neck as I was pushed forward with my captor's free hand.

CHAPTER TWENTY

Widow

My eyes lit up as Frederick brought Julian forward. The only thing that separated me from the cool million that I would gain was his death. Frederick was the man behind the man and my true client; he used Carl as a pawn in his well-thought-out plan. I liked his style. Aasia stood to my right, holding onto her zebra as she looked at Julian without an inch of emotion.

I rarely killed with an audience, but this was becoming something that I relished. Fear lived in his eyes as he glanced at me, but I'd seen that look many times before and it had never stopped me from doing my deed. I just needed Frederick to bring him a little closer. I wanted to see the look in his eye up close as I ended his life.

"Natalie, tell him what's going to happen here tonight." Frederick laughed, as a look of surprise covered Julian's face.

Too bad, he didn't know who his true friends were. If he looked closer, he would've realized the one person that profited from his downfall would be Frederick. Most people displayed loyalty to their own detriment and Julian was no different.

"Tonight, he's going to die," I said as I pulled the knife from inside my sweats.

"Tell him how much I'm going to pay with the money I took from the company," Frederick teased.

"One million dollars..." I laughed, enjoying the sound of those two words as they escaped my mouth.

Julian's eyes were on Aasia. His jaw tightened as he tried not to appear weak for his daughter's sake. He wore the expression of a man looking for the opportunity to save his daughter.

"How about two million?" Frederick asked as he pointed his gun at me.

I didn't understand what was happening. "Yeah, I guess," I said.

"Kill the girl or I'll kill you!" he commanded.

Julian broke free and tried to grab his revolver but was instead hit across the head with the butt of the gun, rendering him bloody. As blood poured from a gash in Julian's head, Frederick kicked him and grabbed him by his neck, pulling his head up to watch.

"You killed my father, so I want you to see your daughter die," Frederick said, slapping him across the face.

I looked down at Aasia while holding the knife in my hand. I realized then that if I had to choose, I would choose her life above mine. I couldn't hurt her nor could I let him hurt her. I stood in front of her as I braced to feel the heat of the gun's bullets.

As he started to pull the trigger, a loud shot rang out and Frederick stumbled to the floor, clutching his heart as steam rose from his shirt. I wasn't surprised at all when I saw the face of his killer.

CHAPTER TWENTY ONE

Julian

I held Aasia tightly in my arms as we descended the stairs. There were news crews everywhere. I could barely believe how quickly they responded to the scene that was unfolding before their eyes.

I could only see out of one eye as Andrea walked ahead of me. Her badge draped around her neck. It gleamed underneath the stars. Natalie was right; Andrea wasn't who she had said she was. She was a federal agent and Noire,Inc. was the target of a government investigation. Frederick had been using the company as his personal washing machine, washing the funds of his underworld friends.

My heart was crushed in more ways than I could fathom at that moment. I liked Andrea a lot, but to know her only purpose in spending time with me was to find incriminating information about me, hurt.

That's why I wasn't surprised when she took Aasia from my arms. The pain coming from the gash was replaced by the throbbing sensation of the handcuffs that were being placed tightly around my wrist. I had told her too much, now I was going to have to find a way to keep my freedom…

CHAPTER TWENTY TWO

Widow

When I hit the streets hours later, I was being hailed as a hero. The hit that Julian sustained had robbed him of most of his short-term memory and he didn't remember why I was even there to begin with. So I was able to walk out of the precinct after a few hours of questioning.

I knew I would have to skip town especially when Natalie and Joull's bodies were discovered. It had been a while since I killed them both and I was sure an odor was beginning to emanate from the walls of his basement. The only problem was that she'd be buried as Garcelle Jean Louis. I needed a new identity and Natalie proved to be the perfect victim. She had no one, so no one would be looking for her.

Frederick also had a friend that I needed to pay a visit. I heard him speaking on the phone and the voice was that of someone I knew all too well. Thomas Willingham Jr. had murdered my only love. Now with a new name and identity, he wouldn't know what hit him…

Continued in the conclusion of the Pleasure Seeker Trilogy "Chocolate City": Hell Hath no Fury like a Woman Scorned.

Please enjoy these sample chapters from **Cater to Her** by Sean Mitchell.

Prologue

ANGELICA
July 8, 2008

My day is finally here. The day I've dreamed about since I was a child living in a Philadelphia orphanage. Never thought it would come, but that has been the norm in my life. I've accomplished more than I ever thought I would. How many orphans do you know that have gone on to graduate top of her class at F.I.T? How many motherless little girls go on to become one of the top Fashion Buyers at Neiman Marcus?

But nothing compares to today, the day of my wedding. It's the day I merge my life with the *perfect* man. Honestly, he's not the *perfect* man, but he's ready and willing to commit, treats me well and earns well into the six figures. I know I come off like some sort of self absorbed, egotistical female, but I'm not. I am just confused and if I don't think about all my groom's good points, I may as well turn around and do a Jackie Joyner Kersee down the aisle.

Everyone's jaws drop as I make my grand entrance. I'm dressed in a Vera Wang wedding gown with a beaded bodice of pearls and sequins. My chapel length train follows me as my eyes begin to water not because of the importance of this occasion, but because of the cameras flashing in my face. They are welcoming me as if they are standing before the Queen of England.

It's almost sacrilegious that I chose to wear white. A color befitting the state of this union would probably be best described as charcoal black or blood red. I'm anything but pure. Over the past month, I've done things even the most promiscuous women would frown upon. I've been in the bed of another man, showered him with my natural juices and put my mouth to every inch of his body. The same mouth I'm about to make a sacred vow with.

I look at all the faces in the crowd as I walk to the wedding march. If they could see my face underneath this veil, they would see a scared girl. This is not the first time these people have seen me with a veil, because I've been wearing the veil of deception for the better part of a month. I see Titus smiling at me, his radiant grin torturing my soul with each hesitant step. That man loves me so much I'm scared I may never measure to the woman he thinks I am.

I locate my best friend Rochelle in the crowd; see the trail of mascara going down her face. She represents the only family I ever had. I'm holding onto my groom's father's arm because there was never a parent in my life to take this walk with me. I know he can feel the vibrations coming from my body because my hands won't stop shaking. My body cannot hide my doubt.

Pastor Richards stands at the pulpit with a self-assured grin on his face. He too is fooled by the lie that my life has become. I finally make it to the altar and intertwine hands with Titus, see the tears congregating by each corner of his eyes. I know in my heart that he loves me even though I can't say the same.

Titus is a beautiful man. With skin the complexion of honey-roasted peanuts, eyes the hue of a Caribbean ocean and lips as full and luscious as a chocolate dipped strawberry. He wasn't just handsome or fine, but rather exceptionally gorgeous. Women could not resist his smile or the way his voice took on a seductive tone whenever he comforted his congregation. He was like a Snapple ice tea, made from the best stuff on earth. And he was mine for the taking, a faithful, trustworthy and hard working man I wasn't sure I really wanted.

When I met Titus at the National Baptist Singles Conference in Richmond, Virginia two years ago, I had no idea he would be the man I married. At the time, I was trying something new. In fact, I considered myself a born again virgin and had put my total trust in Christ to put an end to my insatiable urges. I had come to the conference in search of more bible-based teachings to strengthen my faith and keep me on the straight and narrow.

However, the moment I saw Titus my head filled with thoughts that were anything but holy. When he stepped off the pulpit after a riveting discourse on Singles: respected, successful and spirit filled. I wanted a closer look. He looked sharp, dressed in an immaculate beige Giorgio Armani single-breasted suit. His nails were manicured, eyebrows plucked and his mustache was shaped thin. In other words, metrosexual, just the type of man I loved. Yet, I wasn't the only woman with Reverend Rosemond on her mind as a crowd of admirers gathered around him. He was a scrap of food among ravenous lionesses. There was no ring on his finger and in his sermon; he gave examples of how he as a single man sometimes had difficulty remaining chaste.

It was the last discourse of the day and he was the only reason all the "sisters" were even awake. I couldn't even get within twenty feet as all the "born again virgins" clamored for his attention. Feeling intimidated I left, even though for a millisecond my eyes connected with his. Never to know later I'd meet my fate.

Hours later, I sat alone in the Onyx Lounge, a restaurant in the Marriot Richmond hotel where I was staying. I was dressed down, wearing an oversized Harvard sweatshirt and track pants with my hair pulled back. It's funny, because no matter how much I dressed down to avoid attention from men, they seemed even more aggressive and turned on by my laid-back style.

Men offered me drinks for most of the night and I turned down each and everyone. I didn't want to give anyone an open invitation to hit on me. It was becoming a struggle each and everyday to hold onto my private celibacy vow to God. Sometimes I craved a man's touch so badly I didn't trust myself even to harmlessly converse with the opposite sex.

I hadn't noticed Titus as he sat beside me, but the scent of Grey Flannel instantly caught my attention. My first love wore Grey Flannel, the same man who took my virginity for the first time and as I nursed my drink called, *a goodnight kiss,* I sensed from the corner of my eye someone staring at me.

"You sure know how to light up a room," a familiar voice said.

I was just about to tell him off when we made eye contact for the second time. Usually men of the cloth lack any sense when it comes to fashion. Not to sound condescending but most of them look awkward wearing anything but a suit. Titus proved me wrong; he wore black linen pants, an un-tucked white dress shirt that exposed his glorious pecs and a gold chain with a crucifix. And I couldn't help but look at what he was holding in those slacks.

"Sorry for being rude, but thank you," I said, placing my drink down quickly and putting my hand into my lap. I didn't want him to think I was some type of alcoholic, or worse, yet one of those women that sat in bars picking up men.

"Don't mind me. You know even the Lord had to have a drink from time to time." He laughed, raising his hand to order seltzer water.

I felt uncomfortable, not because I was sitting next to one of God's workers but because my panties were beginning to get moist. His green eyes had a mesmerizing affect on me. And the commanding tone in which he spoke had reverberated from my chest down to my toes. For the first time in four years, I had the urge to pleasure myself. He took one sip of his drink and the site of his lips becoming wet had me wanting to jump him.

"I'm Angelica Thompson. I enjoyed your discourse," I offered him my hand, but he declined.

"I don't mean to be rude sister, but little things such as a hang shake can lead to one of the devils many machinations." He nodded and gulped down the last of his drink.

"I light up a room, but you can't touch me."

"I'm aiming not to touch you physically, but spiritually. Besides I wanted to say thank you for attending my workshop."

"Why thank me?"

Looking at him, I wondered if he resembled an angel. There was not an imperfection on his body, at least not with his clothing on. His skin was clear, his teeth were as white as the wool of a newborn lamb and his hair was curly and fine.

"Unlike everyone else, you seemed to enjoy my workshop. I can tell when a person is listening with more than their ears."

"You speak beautifully. And I need all the help there is."

"And the meek will reside on the earth."

"What do you mean by that?" I asked wondering what our conversation had to do with a scripture from the bible.

"I'm humbled by you. Because I'm sure a single woman as beautiful as you can be doing something more interesting than sitting at a boring workshop. However, you feel a need to be close to God. And that in of itself makes you more attractive."

"I'm nothing to be humbled by," I admitted. If he knew all that I'd been through, if he knew the depths I had gone to get to my station in life, he would've thrown holy water on me.

"Self despair is one of the devil's most potent devices. Whatever you've done and no matter how many times you have sinned, the lord has already forgiven you."

"Tell me Reverend. Why do you even care?"

"Everyday I get on my knees and pray to my wonderful god and I ask him to find someone for me. And everyday he says Titus just a little while longer. This has gone on for years and to be truthful, sister, I was becoming angry in the flesh. But today he answered me." He grabbed a fistful of his shirt, closed his eyes and shook his head.

"And what did he tell you."

"The first will be last and the last will be first. When you left after my workshop I knew…"

"You knew what?"

"I had found my wife…"

Silence had snapped me back from my time warp. The wedding march had ended and now was time to marry this wonderful man. Thinking back to that prophetic day I wondered what Titus had ever seen in me. Two years later and here we are about to get Married and he doesn't even have a clue as to who he's *really* marrying.

"Who gives this woman to be married?" Pastor Richard asks.

"I do," the father of the bride, answers.

In a loud voice Pastor Richard begins, "Welcome family and friends. We meet in this place to celebrate a mystery as ageless as humankind; a mystery of enduring power and inspiration..."

My hands go numb, my legs feel like jelly and I wonder if my lover cares, and if my lover's staring at me. I wonder if my man will stand when the Pastor asks if anyone has a reason why these two shouldn't be married. Will my man forever hold his peace? Will he stand and claim what is his?

Have you ever met a man that is everything you want? I mean a man that looks good, dresses well and can hold a steady J.O.B without a problem, not to mention that in bed he is the equivalent of Michael Jordan on the basketball court or Leonardo Davinci on canvas. Finally yet importantly, gives you orgasms on a mental and spiritual level. I mean when you talk to this extraordinary man the knowledge he imparts is better than the best sex. I've met that man, but it's not the man I'm about to marry...

"Underneath my Skin"

Aurelius

When I think about love, I think of an uncontrollable feeling, a force of nature, one not dictated by our own desires. Its effects are similar to a hurricane that spins us around and around, leaving our destination indiscernible. When you feel it, there's no question. Its power cannot be disputed. Even when lost, its residue reeks on our skin. That's why I fear it. In turn, I avoid it.

There's a great reason as to why I have a great condemnation of it. But I dare not think of it because I could never relive that pain. I loved once and its loss had brought out a side of me I shutter to think of seeing again. The hurt my soul mate inflicted upon me had nearly consumed me, leaving me to wonder if *love* for me even existed. Then I met Mistress Alek and my life changed.

I couldn't see through the leather blindfold, my knees hurt and my backside was in searing pain due to the force of the oak paddle my Dominatrix had pounded me with. And with a slight tug of her leash, the leather collar around my neck tightened and caused me to lose my breath. I could feel her around me, the sound of her heels clicking against the cold linoleum as the braided strands of leather from her flogger lightly touched the hairs of my chest. The scent of warm urine reeked from my skin. That's how she marked me. I was her property. I was her slave and she was my Mistress.

Taking clamps, she began to squeeze my nipples. The pain hurt so good, as I fought a losing battle with the leather of my chastity shorts. She twisted them harder. I held in my screams, bit into the ball gag and began to tear up. I hoped she didn't see the tears filtering down my cheeks. My Mistress would not like it if I appeared weak.

"Are you crying?" My Mistress asked. I shook my head no.

"You're lying to me. And I hate liars," she stated, pulling my leash tightly while digging her heels into my back. I lost my breath once more as the ball gag restricted my breathing. My coughs were hard and shallow. I was beginning to lose circulation in my neck. I gasped, felt nauseous and before I knew it, I could feel no more...

Some consider me perverted, even crazy for the lifestyle that I have chosen. But you have to understand, I get off on pain. That's why my most parts of my anatomy were pierced. And you know what? Each time a sensitive part of my body is pierced my orgasms become even more intense. Therefore, I don't need anyone's pity because the life I live is the life I choose.

If anyone wanted to know the truth about Aurelius, they wouldn't have to look too far back. I took on the name of Aurelius five years ago as an alter ego in the world of S&M. Then two years later, I became Aurelius legally. No last name and no attachments. I was someone before that, had a name and last name that I cringe even to think of. But that boy is dead now, dead with his deep and dark secrets.

Trained as a Personal chef and caterer, I've slaved at some of the finest establishments in the entire world. During my sojourn, I've apprenticed at Ristorante San Domenico in Imola Italy, Stars in Singapore and Gramercy Tavern here in New York City. But after a few too many critiques about my outward appearance, I decided to take my talents elsewhere. And two years later, Foradori catering was born. I provide personal chef services as well as fine catered food. I'm a blue-collar brotha in a white-collar world. I am not rich, at least not yet, but with a few well-placed catering events I hope to be in due time.

Unique would be the best way to describe my personal appearance. You don't see a 6'4 210lbs brotha sporting 8 facial piercings, a 70's style afro and a torso full of tattoos everyday. Even though I've been mistaken for Lenny Kravitz on more than one occasion, people are usually taken aback by my style. My black eyeliner, black finger nail polish and the black threads that I wear have turned a lot of heads, though for the wrong reasons. The only time I wear anything that's not black is when I'm at work.

My favorite pieces of art are on my body. Going up the left side of my torso is a scripture taken from the Holy Qur'an written in the Taliq script form of Arabic Calligraphy, it reads "Thee do we worship, and thine aid do we seek." Around my waist is a barbed wire design and on each of my arms are my parent's pictures along with their days of death for I wasn't scared of death, but embraced it. That's why my favorite color was black.

Getting back to my sex life, I can say honestly that I'm attracted to beautiful women. Don't prejudge me as one of those self-absorbed brothas or one hopelessly into jungle fever. But I can appreciate an attractive white or Asian woman when I see one. Admittedly, back during my wild San Francisco culinary school days, I may have done more than fraternize with a few white girls, even fell in love with a mulatto, but that was then. Now I like my sistas and haven't had an urge to go back to the light side. At least, not since… *her*.

Sitting in the sauna of the Harlem New York sports club after an hour session of Yoga, I was exhausted. I leaned against the wooden walls with my eyes closed trying to sweat out all the negative energy that resided in my body from another busy catering affair. This was my normal Sunday routine. After a hectic week, it provided me with a sense of peace. Besides, I was alone. Since I liked to whisk in the nude, the other men in the club didn't share a sauna with me. The sight of another dude swinging from side to side put off most brothas.

It didn't take long before the mouth of my best friend Shane disturbed my peace. Shane Hildebrand is what I like to call unapologetically gay. He reveled in his gayness, the complete opposite of the down low brotha. He's the on top brotha, as in on top of a mountain screaming to the entire world that he's gay and loves it.

Shane is sort of a cross between Sisqo and Little Richard. He's beanpole skinny, all legs and arms and walks with a switch. His low-cropped hair is dyed blond and topped off with glitter because he likes his head to shimmer. His mustache, goatee and sideburns are all cut razor thin,

Shane knew me better than anyone ever knew me. Hell, he even knew my real name. I've known him since our San Francisco days when I attended The California Culinary Academy and he attended San Francisco State. Back then, we thought we were all that, having unprotected sex with as many people as the law allowed. But I never really warmed up to that life. Ignorant as I was, I actually thought there was someone out there that was especially made for me.

Speaking of Shane, there is no building, no matter the amount of floors that can hold his ego. He has his own tailored suit salon in Saks Fifth Avenue. And compared to his couture, all other high-end fashion is considered "trash" in his mind. If he as much as caught me with anything that didn't bear the Marcus Jacobs name, he would give me an hour-long lecture on the near extinction of black designers. Good thing I was naked underneath this towel, because I didn't want to hear it.

"You can start living because Mrs. Shane is in the building," Shane cooed strutting into the sauna in full America's next top model mode. Shane never ceased to amaze me as he entered without a towel, which is usually required attire when walking from the locker room into the sauna.

"It's just a matter of time before they kick your butt out into the street," I interjected.

"This pretty behind? Why would they do a thing like that? I add style to this place. And you know style isn't bought. It's born."

"Well, I know one thing; you're gonna buy yourself a one way ticket out onto the sidewalk."

"You're just being a drama queen," Shane responded, sitting down across from me with his legs crossed. "And just for that remark I'm not even gonna give you a peek of my goodies."

Shane was like a heterosexual brotha, always thinking with his smaller head and not his big head. Ever since he had a rendezvous with one of the yoga instructors in the very sauna, he's been putting his goods on display, hoping to probably score another or two.

"Getting desperate because your yoga friend ain't giving you the time of day?" I laughed, tossing him my extra towel and closing my eyes again. His hot room fling turned out to be very married and heavily in denial.

"Hell, he's still giving me a little sumtin, sumtin."

"He actually has the time, when he's not with his wife and two kids," I replied sarcastically, peeking through one eye to gauge his distaste. It wasn't like me to take pleasure in another person's pain, but I knew Shane. If he wasn't getting it from one place, he was damn sure getting it from another.

"Well, at least I have a love life. You need to dust off that python between your legs and get back into the jungle," Shane retorted.

My double life in S&M was even a secret to Shane. Not because he wouldn't take pleasure in my activities, but because some were even too hardcore for his taste. That's why I always kept two or three towels at my disposal, to cover up all the black and blues courtesy of my Mistress. I stood up and draped one towel over my waist and the other over my back to hide any evidence of last night. As I proceeded to the sauna door, I stopped in my tracks and thought about what Shane had said.

"You're right. I don't have a love life because there's no such thing as love." I laughed, but not in a funny manner. Shane shook his head, obviously annoyed by my constant negativity. "See you later biyotch."

I had just moved into *The Lenox* condominiums only a month prior, but had already had several complaints levied against me. My apartment was on the 12th floor and I had use of my very own roof top terrace. And I loved to walk around my condo in the nude, whether to enjoy the humidity outside or listen to some *Najee* while drinking a glass of red wine. However, my carefree lifestyle obviously ruffled a few feathers in the tenement building across the street because I was warned by the building superintendent to be more discreet. Still, I didn't see anything wrong in putting my chiseled frame on show in the confines of my home. I would've thought Harlem was a little more tolerant than those rich stiffs on the Eastside. As the sun went down, a cool breeze found its way into the open terrace doors. I stood on my patio clothed in only a silk robe as I sort relaxation by way of a little hash. Below, I could hear meringue infused music coming from a fruit truck idling by. The pit of my stomach got a little queasy as I looked down. Reminded me of the times my father would throw me in the air when I was a child. The only fond memory I ever had of him.

Thinking about my parents usually caused my eyes to well. They both died in a carbon monoxide accident only two years after they banished me from their home. Regretfully, I never got the chance to apologize for something I couldn't control. Hindsight is twenty, twenty and if I knew what I know now the love of another would have never been worth the love of my parents.

I took a seat on my Teak wood chaise and took a heavy drag of my herbal ecstasy. I love the excitement that New York exudes, but when looking into the atmosphere you cannot locate one damn star. That's what I miss about Memphis. I grew up in the predominantly white suburb of Collierville, Tennessee, the token black in a sea of white faces.   Underneath the southern sky, there was always time for peace. My mother and I would sit on our porch over a pitcher of homemade sun tea and talk about the future.

I was small then and she would hold me in her arms and look into my eyes with a face that reflected mine. They called her pretty Millie, because her skin was the hue of Milk and honey and her eyes were like radiant orbs of gold. Just by smiling she could light up a room and with a shake of her hip could send men to the hospital emergency room with neck injuries.

And she was a great listener, one of the many qualities that I inherited from her. No matter what I told her I wanted to be, regardless of its difficulty, she would always say, "I know you will." Sometimes I longed for her assurances, though I'm happy with how my life has evolved. I still wonder if I would've made her proud.

After finishing off my joint, I decided to go to bed and prepare for another day at the office. As much as I loved food preparation, its fast-paced nature was beginning to take its toll. With the money I made since starting my business, I could start my own restaurant and move away to somewhere hot.

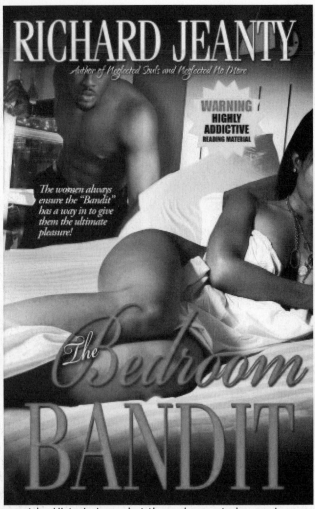

It may not be Histeria Lane, but these desperate housewives are fed up with their neglecting husbands. Their sexual needs take precedence over the millions of dollars their husbands bring home every year to keep them happy in their affluent neighborhood. While their husbands claim to be hard at work, these wives are doing a little work of their own with the bedroom bandit. Is the bandit swift enough to evade these angry husbands?

In Stores!!

NEGLECTED SOULS

Motherhood and the trials of loving too hard and not enough frame
this story...The realism of these characters will bring tears to your
spirit as you discover the hero in the villain you never saw coming...
Neglected Souls is a gritty, honest and heart-stirring story of hope and
personal triumph set in the ghettos of Boston.

In Stores!!!

Jimmy and Nina continue to feel a void in their lives because they
haven't a clue about their genealogical make-up. Jimmy falls victims
to a life threatening illness and only the right organ donor can save his
life. Will the donor be the bridge to reconnect Jimmy and Nina to
their biological family? Will Nina be the strength for her brother in
his time of need? Will they ever find out what really happened to their
mother?

In Stores!!!

Betrayal, lust, lies, murder, deception, sex and tainted love frame this story... Julian Stevens lacks the ambition and freak ability that Miko looks for in a man, but she married him despite his flaws to spite an ex-boyfriend. When Miko least expects it, the old boyfriend shows up and ready to sweep her off her feet again. She wants to have her cake and eat it too. While Miko's doing her own thing, Julian is determined to become everything Miko ever wanted in a man and more, but will he go to extreme lengths to prove he's worthy of Miko's love? Julian Stevens soon finds out that he's capable of being more than he could ever imagine as he embarks on a journey that will change his life forever.

In Stores!!!

The police in New York and other major cities around the country are increasingly victimizing black men. The violence has escalated to deadly force, most of the time without justification. In this controversial book, noted author Richard Jeanty, tackles the problem of police brutality and the unfair treatment of Black men at the hands of police in New York City and the rest of the country.

In Stores!!!

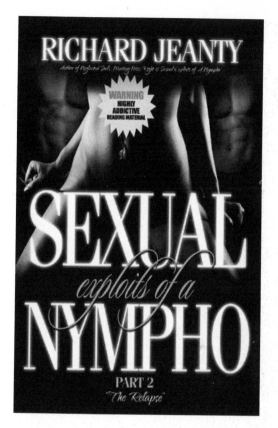

Just when Darren thinks his relationship with Tina is flourishing, there is yet another hurdle on the road hindering their bliss. Tina saw a therapist for months to deal with her sexual addiction, but now Darren is wondering if she was ever treated completely. Darren has not been taking care of home and Tina's frustrated and agrees to a break-up with Darren. Will Darren lose Tina for good? Will Tina ever realize that Darren is the best man for her?

In Stores!!

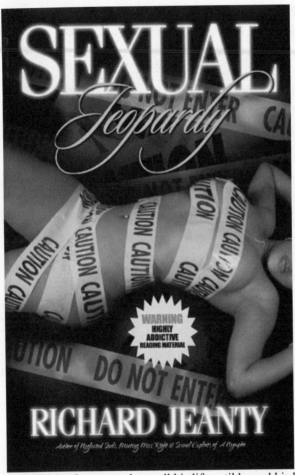

Ronald Murphy was a player all his life until he and his best friend, Myles, met the women of their dreams during a brief vacation in South Beach, Florida. Sexual Jeopardy is story of trust, betrayal, forgiveness, friendship and hope.

In Stores!!!

Tina develops an insatiable sexual appetite very early in life. She only loves her boyfriend, Darren, but he's too far away in college to satisfy her sexual needs.

Tina decides to get buck wild away in college

Will her sexual trysts jeopardize the lives of the men in her life?

In Stores!!!

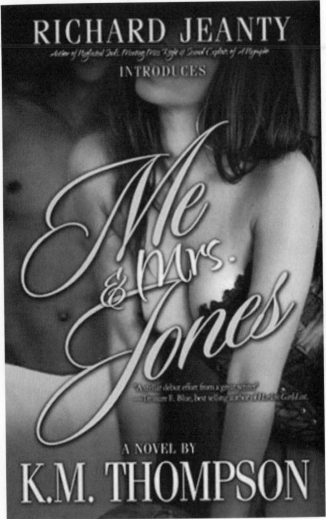

Faith Jones, a woman in her mid-thirties, has given up on ever finding love again until she met her son's best friend, Darius. Faith Jones is walking a thin line of betrayal against her son for the love of Darius. Will Faith allow her emotions to outweigh her common sense?

In Stores!!!

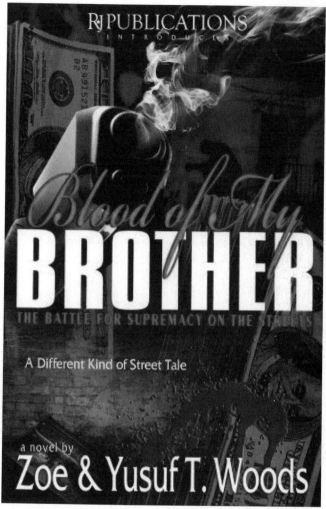

Roc was the man on the streets of Philadelphia, until his younger brother decided it was time to become his own man by wreaking havoc on Roc's crew without any regards for the blood relation they share. Drug, murder, mayhem and the pursuit of happiness can lead to deadly consequences. This story can only be told by a person who has lived it.

In Stores!!!

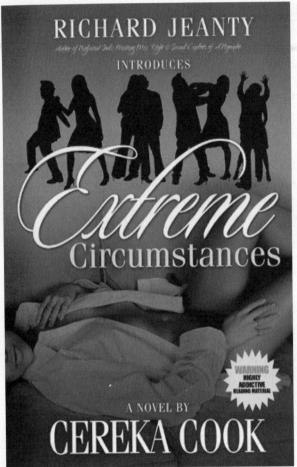

What happens when a devoted woman is betrayed? Come take a ride with Chanel as she takes her boyfriend, Donnell, to circumstances beyond belief after he betrays her trust with his endless infidelities. How long can Chanel's friend, Janai, use her looks to get what she wants from men before it catches up to her? Find out as Janai's gold-digging ways catch up with and she has to face the consequences of her extreme actions.

In Stores!!!

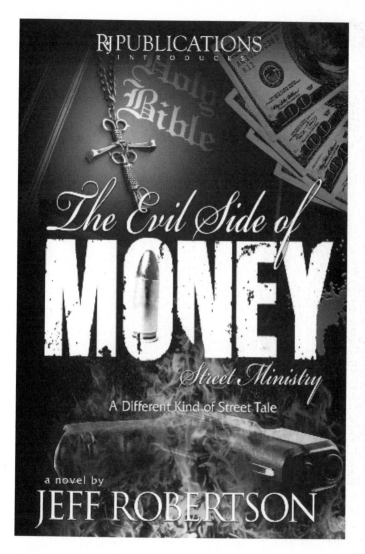

Violence, Intimidation and carnage are the order as Nathan and his
brother set out to build the most powerful drug empires in Chicago.
However, when God comes knocking, Nathan's conscience starts to
surface. Will his haunted criminal past get the best of him?

In Stores!!

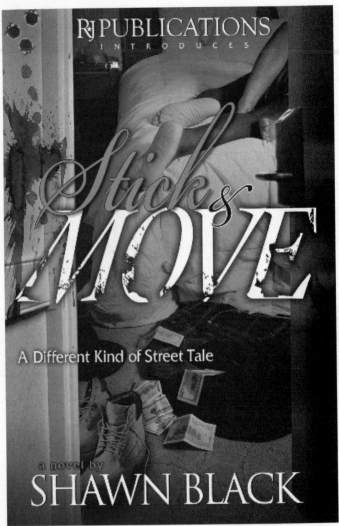

Yasmina witnessed the brutal murder of her parents at a young age at the hand of a drug dealer. This event stained her mind and upbringing as a result. Will Yamina's life come full circle with her past? Find out as Yasmina's crew, The Platinum Chicks, set out to make a name for themselves on the street.

In stores!!

Ashland's mother, Bianca, fights hard to suppress the truth from her daughter because she doesn't want her to marry Jordan, the grandson of an ex-lover she loathes. Ashland soon finds out how cruel and vengeful her mother can be, but what price will Bianca pay for redemption?

In stores!!

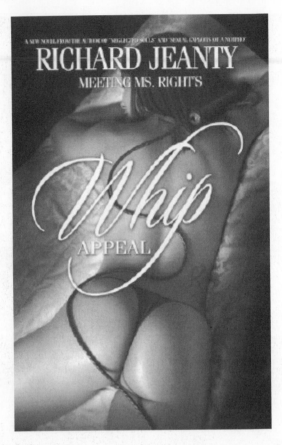

Malcolm is a wealthy virgin who decides to conceal his wealth From the world until he meets the right woman. His wealthy best friend, Dexter, hides his wealth from no one. Malcolm struggles to find love in an environment where vanity and materialism are rampant, while Dexter is getting more than enough of his share of women. Malcolm needs develop self-esteem and confidence to meet the right woman and Dexter's confidence is borderline arrogance.
Will bad boys like Dexter continue to take women for a ride?

Or will nice guys like Malcolm continue to finish last?

In Stores!!!

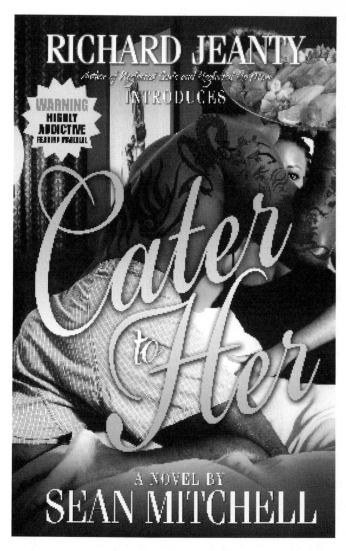

What happens when a woman's devotion to her fiancee is tested weeks before she gets married? What if her fiancee is just hiding behind the veil of ministry to deceive her? Find out as Sean Mitchell takes you on a journey you'll never forget into the lives of Angelica, Titus and Aurelius.

In Stores!!

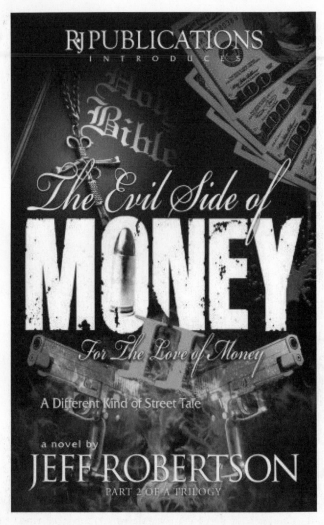

A beautigul woman from Bolivia threatens the existence of the drug empire that Nate and G have built. While Nate is head over heels for her, G can see right through her. As she brings on more conflict between the crew, G sets out to show Nate exactly who she is before she brings about their demise.

In Stores!!!

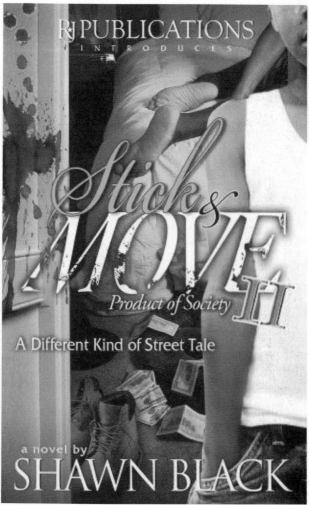

Scorcher and Yasmina's low key lifestyle was interrupted when they were taken down by the Feds, but their daughter, Serosa, was left to be raised by the foster care system. Will Serosa become a product of her environment or will she rise above it all? Her bloodline is undeniable, but will she be able to control it?

In Stores!!

RJ PUBLICATIONS
INTRODUCES

Flippin' The

GAME

A Different Kind of Street Tale

a novel by

ALETHEA & MYLES RAMZEE

An ex-drug dealer finds himself in a bind after he's caught by the Feds. He has to decide which is more important, his family or his loyalty to the game. As he fights hard to make a decision, those who helped him to the top fear the worse from him. Will he get the chance to tell the govt. whole story, or will someone get to him before he becomes a snitch?

In Stores!!!

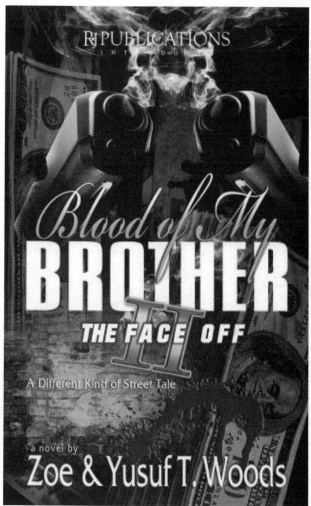

What will Roc do when he finds out the true identity of Solo? Will the blood shed come from his own brother Lil Mac? Will Roc and Solo take their beef to an explosive height on the street? Find out as Zoe and Yusuf bring the second installment to their hot street joint, Blood of My Brother.

In Stores!!!

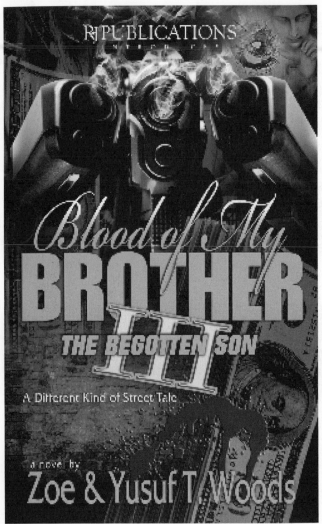

The strategic game of chess that began with the pushing of a pawn in the Blood of My Brother series, symbolizes one of love, loyalty, blood, mayhem and death. Who will be the one to announce checkmate between the two kings left standing; the teacher or the student?

Coming August 2009

Dave Richardson is enjoying success as his second book became a New York Times best-seller. He left the life of The Bedroom behind to settle with his family, but an obsessed fan has not had enough of Dave and she will go to great length to get a piece of him. How far will a woman go to get a man that doesn't belong to her?

Coming September 2010

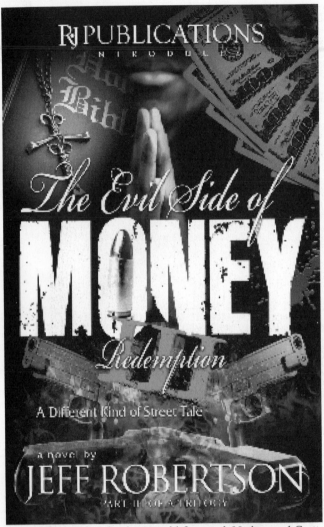

Forced to abandon the drug world for good, Nathan and G attempt to change their lives and move forward, but will their past come back to haunt them? This final installment will leave you speechless.

Coming November 2009

Nafys Muhammad managed to beat the charges in court, but will he beat them on the street? There will be many revelations in this story as betrayal, greed, sex scandal corruption and murder unravels throughout every page. Get ready for a rough ride.

Coming December 2009

Deon is at the mercy of a ruthless gang that kidnapped him. In a foreign land where he knows nothing about the culture, he has to use his survival instincts and his wit to outsmart his captors. Will the Hoodfellas show up in time to rescue Deon, or will Crazy D take over once again and fight an all out war by himself?

Coming March 2010

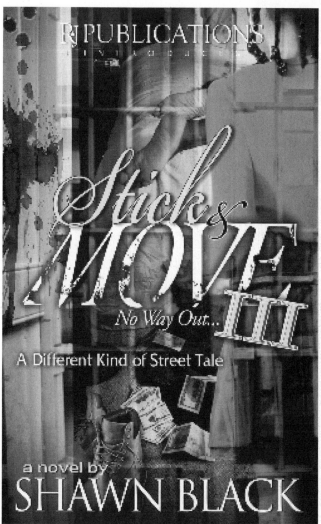

While Yasmina sits on death row awaiting her fate, her daughter, Serosa, is fighting the fight of her life on the outside. Her genetic structure that indirectly bins her to her parents could also be her downfall and force her to see that there's no way out!

Coming January 2010

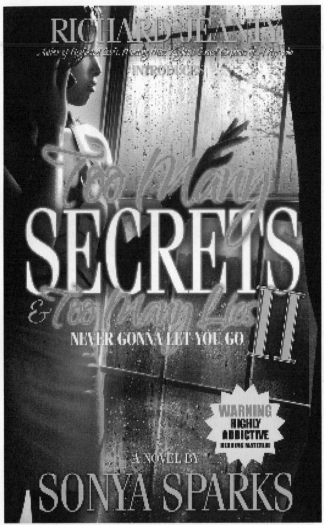

The drama continues as Deshun is hunted by Angela who still feels that ex-girlfriend Kayla is still trying to win his heart, though he brutally raped her. Angela will kill anyone who gets in her way, but is DeShun worth all the aggravation?

Coming September 2009

Buck Johnson was forced to make the best out of worst situation. He has witnessed the most cruel events in his life and it is those events who the man that he has become. Was the Johnson family ignorant souls through no fault of their own?

Coming October 2009

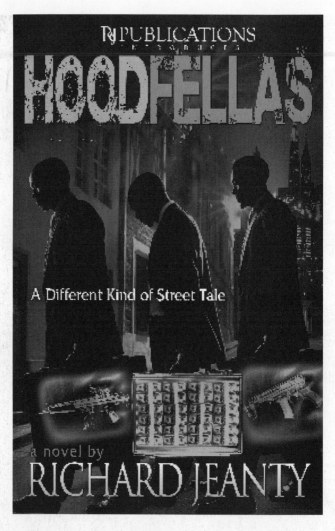

When an Ex-con finds himself destitute and in dire need of the basic necessities after he's released from prison, he turns to what he knows best, crime, but at what cost? Extortion, murder and mayhem drives him back to the top, but will he stay there?

In Stores !!!

What happens when someone falls insanely in love? Stalking is just the beginning.

In Stores!!!

B or Q Train

Miami Noire   *W.S. Burkett*

to Brighton Beach

PUBLICATIONS
BRINGING EXCITEMENT, FUN AND JOY TO READING

31 to

Oriental Blvd Use this coupon to order by mail

1. Neglected Souls, Richard Jeanty $14.95
2. Neglected No More, Richard Jeanty $14.95
3. Sexual Exploits of Nympho, Richard Jeanty $14.95
4. Meeting Ms. Right's Whip Appeal, Richard Jeanty $14.95
5. Me and Mrs. Jones, K.M Thompson ($14.95) Available
6. Chasin' Satisfaction, W.S Burkett ($14.95) Available
7. Extreme Circumstances, Cereka Cook ($14.95) Available
8. The Most Dangerous Gang In America, R. Jeanty $15.00
9. Sexual Exploits of a Nympho II, Richard Jeanty $15.00
10. Sexual Jeopardy, Richard Jeanty $14.95 Coming: 2/15/ 2008
11. Too Many Secrets, Too Many Lies, Sonya Sparks $15.00
12. Stick And Move, Shawn Black ($15.00) Coming 1/15/ 2008
13. Evil Side Of Money, Jeff Robertson $15.00
14. Cater To Her, W.S Burkett $15.00 Coming 3/30/ 2008
15. Blood of my Brother, Zoe & Ysuf Woods $15.00
16. Hoodfellas, Richard Jeanty $15.00 11/30/2008
17. The Bedroom Bandit, Richard Jeanty $15.00 March 2009
18. Stick N Move II, Shawn Black $15.00 April 2009
19. Miami Noire, W.S. Burkett $15.00 June 2009
20. Insanely In Love, Cereka Cook $15.00 May 2009
21. Blood of My Brother III, Zoe & Yusuf Woods August 2009

Name_____

Address_____

City_____State_____Zip Code_____

Please send the novels that I have circled above.

Shipping and Handling: Free
Total Number of Books_____
Total Amount Due_____

Buy 3 books and get 1 free. This offer is subject to change without notice.

Send institution check or money order (no cash or CODs) to:
RJ Publications
PO Box 300771
Jamaica, NY 11434

For more information please call 718-471-2926, or visit www.rjpublications.com

Please allow 2-3 weeks for delivery.